DODGER BOY

DODGER BOY

Sarah Ellis

Groundwood Books
House of Anansi Press
Toronto Berkeley

Groundwood Books / House of Anansi Press
groundwoodbooks.com

We acknowledge for their financial support of our publishing program the Canada
Council for the Arts, the Ontario Arts Council and the Government of Canada.

 Canada Council **Conseil des Arts**
for the Arts **du Canada**

 ONTARIO ARTS COUNCIL
CONSEIL DES ARTS DE L'ONTARIO
an Ontario government agency
un organisme du gouvernement de l'Ontario

With the participation of the Government of Canada
Avec la participation du gouvernement du Canada | Canadä

Library and Archives Canada Cataloguing in Publication
Ellis, Sarah, author
Dodger boy / Sarah Ellis.
Issued in print and electronic formats.
ISBN 978-1-77306-072-9 (hardcover).—ISBN 978-1-77306-073-6 (HTML).—
ISBN 978-1-77306-092-7 (Kindle)
I. Title.
PS8559.L57D63 2018   JC813'.54   C2018-900057-0
                        C2018-900058-9

Cover design by Michael Solomon
Cover art copyright © 2018 by Aimée Sicuro

Groundwood Books is committed to protecting our natural environment. As part
of our efforts, the interior of this book is printed on paper that contains 100%
post-consumer recycled fibers, is acid-free and is processed chlorine-free.

Printed and bound in Canada

MIX
Paper from
responsible sources
FSC® C016245

For Circle Dot with love and gratitude

one

It all started with *Romeo and Juliet*, the movie. It was Charlotte's idea but Dawn took some convincing.

"Is it going to be weird English or normal?"

"Well, Shakespeare."

"I don't think so."

"Come on, Dawn. It's romance. You saw the poster. Greatest love story of all time and all that. Plus that theater has real butter on the popcorn."

The popcorn did it.

The movie didn't start out that well. The first problem was the way the men dressed, with leotards and those flaps covering their crotches. Charlotte was doing her best to be cool, but really! One nudge from Dawn and she was off into squished-down giggles.

Then there was a bunch of fighting, with idiot boys spitting on one another and then practically killing each other with swords. It was like the boys' side of the playground at recess. Familiar but — snoresville.

Then Juliet's mother appeared and she was wearing this silver helmet thing on her head. Dawn leaned over and whispered, "Bubblehead," and that was it for Charlotte. Giggle explosion disguised as coughing. Charlotte could feel the dirty looks from other moviegoers beaming through the dark.

This was just the sort of thing that she hated — acting like an obnoxious teenager in public. This was just the sort of thing that had prompted the Unteen Pact, an agreement that she and Dawn made last January when they turned thirteen — an agreement to refuse to become teenagers.

Concentrating on the sadness of world hunger diluted the giggles for a few seconds, and then Juliet's mother appeared in yet another metal beehive and Charlotte and Dawn were off again.

All that ended when Romeo went to a masked ball. It was eyes meeting across a crowded room and you could see them falling in love, every second of the slow fall. Romeo went round and round the room trying to catch a glimpse of Juliet and from that moment Charlotte was hooked. They were both so beautiful. Well, Juliet more than Romeo, actually. Romeo seemed a bit wimpy with odd hair. But Juliet! Charlotte had never really thought about what "heart-shaped face" meant before.

By the time it was over and practically everyone was dead, Charlotte was crying and she heard a little sob beside her. Luckily she was well stocked with Kleenex. Dawn was an elegant crier but Charlotte was a snotty one and needed to mop up.

It seemed all wrong to emerge into a glaring busy Saturday afternoon outside, car horns and sunshine and people who couldn't care less about Romeo and Juliet and the terrible tragedy of love.

"I'm *so* glad you made me come," said Dawn. "You know what's the most amazing thing? She was *thirteen*. Did you get that?"

"But so Unteen."

Dawn frowned. "You think?"

"Absolutely. Apply the formula."

The formula had been invented by Charlotte, with Dawn's input, to explain the bizarre behavior of boy-crazy girls acting fake-stupid — a phenomenon they had noticed at school and that was part of the motivation for the Unteen Pact.

Dawn pushed the Walk button. "Okay. Part one: obviously zero percent."

Part one of the formula was status, the way you could show off if you had a boyfriend and get popularity points. Dawn and Charlotte figured that for most of the girls at school this was the whole deal. A high score on part one was clear proof of teen-silly.

"Right. Romeo and Juliet aren't going around bragging to their friends. They can't because of the whole family mess. Plus Juliet just isn't the type. Remember that bit where she tells Romeo straight out that she isn't going to flirt and play hard to get? She's smart and she doesn't pretend not to be. I think she might be the hero of the Unteen movement."

"Right. Part two: ringy-dingy."

Ringy-dingy was wanting to get married so you could have a house and babies and a dinette suite and all that. A high score on part two was pathetic.

Charlotte dodged a wheelchair barreling up the sidewalk. "But they *do* get married."

"But not for the dinette suite. I think that's zero percent as well."

"Yeah. I mean, Bubblehead tries to marry her off but Juliet would rather die than marry that Paris guy. You're right. Zero. So that leaves part three."

Part three was kissing, etc., etc.

Dawn grinned. "I'd say one hundred percent! They were so hot for each other."

"But then there's no percent for the Big One."

Part four, the Big One, was the once-in-a-lifetime romance, the lightning bolt that changed you forever and led to heroic acts, wild behavior and writing poetry.

"There was a lot about the Big One. They said they were each other's *souls*. You have to give part four at least fifty percent."

"Okay, sex and love. So the total score for Romeo and Juliet is zero, zero, fifty, fifty."

"Perfect score."

Dawn paused at a shoestore window. "Wouldn't it be great to have somebody look at you like Romeo stared at Juliet?"

"I don't know. I think it would make me feel like I had spinach between my teeth."

"Charlotte Quintan! You're a goof! It would be love, not spinach. The adoring gaze. That's what everybody wants, deep down."

Charlotte stared at the shoes and wondered. Was that what she wanted, deep down? Dawn was always so sure of herself. It was one of her best things.

"Okay, shopping game. You get to have any of the shoes in the window. One, two, three, point."

"Hang on. Give me a minute to look!"

"One, two, three, go!"

Same choice. Separated at birth. Or it might have been Shakespeare. The green suede shoes with little green leather buttons were like something Juliet would wear.

"Want, want, double-want," Dawn sighed. "Let's go in and see how much they are."

"No, if it's the kind of place where they don't put on the prices it will be way out of our zone."

"Zone! We're so broke we don't even have a zone."

"Exactly. They'll know we're not serious."

"So?"

"You go ahead. I'll just stay out here."

Charlotte looked through the window and across the display and saw Dawn chatting away to the sales clerk who actually took the shoes out of the display to show her. They talked for a few more minutes and then seemed to part best friends and Dawn reappeared on the sidewalk.

"So?"

"Don't even ask. Italian. Hand-sewn. You should have seen them close up. They even smelled delicious. We have *such* good taste, you and me."

Dawn could do that, thought Charlotte. She could walk into a store and talk to a sales clerk without rehearsing in her head. Charlotte couldn't even imagine it.

{|}

Dawn was the one to spot the poster on the telephone pole.

"Hey, what's that about?"

It was in bright psychedelic colors, crazy swoopy shapes and fat balloon lettering.

Easter Human Be-In
Second Beach
Easter Sunday
Ecto-Plasmic Assault Light Show
Mother Tucker's Yellow Duck
Peace Love Music
Free to All Humans

Charlotte read it twice. Ecto-plasmic wasn't the only mystery.

"What does be-in mean?"

"Charlotte, get with it, it's a joke. Like human being, human be-in."

"I get that. But what do you actually *do* at a be-in?"

"One way to find out. We should go. It says free."

"What about if it's just for hippies?"

"Look. Free to all humans. That means us. Plus, we could be hippies for the day. Why not? It's all about the clothes."

Why not was another of Dawn's best things. By the time they turned off Robson Street they had a well-designed plan to spend the weekend on a hippie-disguise project.

TWO

Groovy Tie-Dye Fun. Charlotte flipped through the library book.

"Is this the look we really want? We could just do normal plus a headband and beads or something."

"But this is groovy! Look, it says so right on the cover. Library books don't lie. Don't you want to be groovy?"

"Oh, good grief. Who really says groovy?"

Dawn grinned. "Well, nobody. But maybe they do in, like, San Francisco and other real hippie places. Why not? It's just for one day. And tie-dye looks like fun."

It did look like fun. And making it didn't mean you actually had to wear it. "Okay."

"Great! Let's make a list of what we need. Fabric, dye, salt, colored chalk, rubber gloves, elastic bands ... Hmmmm. I think we'll have to do it at your house."

"Well, I guess!" Charlotte glanced around the Novaks' living room. The coffee table matched the stereo matched the china cabinet. There was a color scheme of avocado green and harvest gold. There were ornaments. One perfect shiny philodendron sat in a perfect shiny pot. There was absolutely no clutter. Mr. and Mrs. Novak went in for interior decoration.

Charlotte's parents had apparently never heard of interior decoration. There was furniture, obviously, and rugs and curtains and pictures on the walls, but it was hard to imagine that anybody had ever actually chosen the stuff. It just seemed to be there, a kind of festival of clutter. There were plants, of course — plants from asparagus to zebrina — but mostly they were ailing.

The family business was a plant store, Green Thumb. If a plant wasn't doing well it came home to recover. It drove Charlotte's brother crazy.

"Throw them out! It's called stock shrinkage." James was at university studying business and he liked to say things like "stock shrinkage."

Charlotte loved the calm order of Dawn's house. When she had her own place it was going to be matchy just like that. But she did have to admit that Villa Quintan was better for projects, especially messy ones.

She turned over a page in the book.

"White all-cotton fabric recommended. What are we going to use? T-shirts?"

"I don't know. You don't see hippie girls wearing T-shirts so much. They seem, you know, flouncier."

Charlotte did a quick mental inventory of her closet.

"I don't think I have flouncy."

"Me neither. Time for a trip to the Sally Ann."

{I}

The Salvation Army Thrift Store made Charlotte think of archeology. At first it looked like there was nothing there. A dusty hillside in Egypt. Just racks and racks of pilled brown cardigans and saggy shirts and that funny sweet smell.

But somewhere in there was King Tut's golden treasure, especially if you were there with Dawn.

Flip, reject. Flip, reject. Flip, reject. Dawn walked her fingers through the hangers.

"Okay. Bad. Good but not for the be-in. Maybe. Ick. Polyester. Now *here's* a possibility."

Dawn held up a long white skirt with a row of small bells around the waist. "Indian cotton, unbleached, drawstring waist, not stinky, nice touch of hippie. Now we're getting somewhere. Hold this."

Charlotte took the skirt and wandered over to a shelf of books. She was just cracking one open when Dawn reappeared.

"Charlotte! Keep focused. Don't start reading. Look what I found. Another perfect skirt. We're set. We can pair the skirts with maybe a blouse or a plain T-shirt. Or maybe one each. We don't want to look too twinny."

"Do we need to try them on?"

"Nah. Drawstring waists. One size fits all."

Charlotte followed Dawn to the cash desk. She was just digging out her wallet when Dawn stopped dead in her tracks.

"Is that …?" She grabbed Charlotte by the sleeve and pulled her toward a rack that was half-hidden behind the door.

"Holy cow!" she whispered. She pulled out a dress of layers of creamy lace and checked the label.

"I knew it! Laura Ashley. She shoots, she scores."

She glanced around. "Look at the price. They don't know what they've got. Be cool."

Charlotte ran her hand over the fabric. It *was* beautiful, soft and heavy. She imagined how it would hang and move.

"Why would somebody even give this away?"

Dawn's x-ray eyes found the answer. "Look. Stain. Somebody had an accident with a felt-tip marker."

"But who cares? We'll tie-dye over it. Right?"

"Exactly! So now we only need one of the skirts. Which one do you want, bells or no bells?"

A flicker of hurt flashed through Charlotte. The lace dress obviously wasn't for her. "So. Um. Maybe I'll wear the dress?"

Dawn shook her head and put her hand on Charlotte's arm. "Oh, that wouldn't work. Laura Ashley just isn't you."

"No?"

"Definitely not. You're earthier. You should pick the skirt with the bells. I'll lend you that peasant blouse I have, the one with the embroidery. That will be a much better look for you."

Earthier? Oh, well. Dawn was probably right. She was good at fashion.

And at bargaining. Most people didn't bargain at the Sally Ann. Things were cheap enough even for those with no zone. But Dawn pointed out the stain on the dress and got a cheerful discount.

{1}

The plan was to dye on Saturday morning. But Charlotte had not predicted a competing project of homemade lasagna noodles. She stumbled into the kitchen, rubbing sleep out of her eyes, to find her mother and Uncle Claude hanging sheets of pasta over the backs of chairs.

"Claude! You're back."

Claude clapped flour off his hands and surrounded Charlotte with a hug. His beard tickled. "Got in late last night."

"You don't want to take a rest from cooking?"

Mom shook her head. "He's crazy."

"Lots of time to rest when you're six feet under. I just got this idea to make lasagna noodles. The loggers don't appreciate such subtleties."

Uncle Claude worked as a cook in lumber camps and lived with Charlotte's family when he wasn't in the bush. Mom told Charlotte that he'd been in lots of trouble when he was young, in jail and all that.

"Nowadays they'd probably call him hyperactive but back then they just called him a juvenile delinquent."

"So what's my favorite niece up to today?"

"Um, Dawn and I were going to tie-dye."

"Tie die. What's that? No, let me guess." Claude pretended to strangle himself. "That would be dying from being forced to wear a tie every day. Is there anything as ridiculous as a tie? Who invented it? What use is it?"

Charlotte remembered her Girl Guides first-aid training.

"Well, in an emergency in the woods you can use it as a tourniquet, or to make a temporary splint with a branch. If you break your leg or something."

"But who would be out in the woods wearing a tie?"

In a piece of perfect comic timing, James walked into the kitchen. He was wearing chinos, a button-down shirt and a tie.

Charlotte raised her eyebrows. "Um." Mom and Claude laughed.

"What?" said James, frowning.

"Nothing," said Claude. "Where are you off to today?"

"Hey, Claude. Welcome home. I'm going out to school. Saturday seminar in business math. Is there any coffee?"

Charlotte stared at James as he took a mug off the drainboard. Coffee and ties. He had become a mysterious stranger since he started university

"Anyway," said Claude. "Death by ties. I get it."

"Actually it's not dying as in death but dyeing as in adding color."

"What are you planning to dye?" asked Mom.

"A skirt and a dress. Dawn and me? We're making costumes for the Human Be-In next weekend in Stanley Park."

"Human being?" asked Mom.

James rolled his eyes. "Bunch of dope-smoking hippie loser long-hairs."

"Now, James, no need to be narrow-minded. Are you having breakfast before you go?"

James flinched, shook his head, and carried his coffee out the door.

"I guess budding businessmen don't eat breakfast," said Mom.

"So we need some plastic buckets that it doesn't matter if they get wrecked."

"Problem is," said Mom, "that I can't see pasta-making and tie-dyeing going on in the same kitchen at once."

The kitchen door opened and Dawn appeared, backing in with her arms full of bags.

"Hi, everybody. Claude! You're back. What's that stuff hanging on the chairs?"

"Maybe tie-dye could happen outside? Under the deck?" said Claude.

"But we need hot water."

"Coffee urn do you? I can get it from the garage. And there's some buckets there, too."

"Don't dye the urn, okay? We need it tomorrow for Meeting and I don't want to give them blue coffee," said Mom.

{|}

Under the deck was crowded with stuff.

Charlotte sighed, "This family is hopeless. Your parents would never keep a rusty barbecue 'just in case.'"

"But I love all your stuff." Dawn put down an armful of bags and edged a faded pink plastic box from under the chaos.

"Look! L'il Kitchen. I remember this." She opened up the L'il Oven and pulled out a stuffed animal. "Pandabear! Oh. He's not looking too good."

"Ick! He's not only moldy. He's suppurating."

Dawn rolled her eyes. "Suppurating! Word Power, right?"

Charlotte was a loyal reader of "It Pays to Increase Your Word Power" in *Reader's Digest*.

"Yup, good one, eh? Sounds like it means. Okay. Let's get things set up. Here's the rubber gloves. The plug for the urn is behind that piece of plywood."

By piling, rearranging and hucking they were able to clear a space. They set up the buckets on some garden chairs and balanced the coffee urn on a plastic milk crate. *Groovy Tie-Dye Fun* was propped on a pile of plant pots.

Dawn tore open the packets of dye. "Red, yellow, blue. We should be able to make all the colors. Is the water hot yet?"

"Use lots of dye. Groovy says we want intense color."

"Okay. Step one. Twist your garment into a spiral."

The girls squinched up the wet skirt and dress and tied them into lumps.

Out of the corner of her eye, Charlotte noticed the chair holding the bucket of blue beginning to rock on the uneven ground.

"Hey! Puff! Get off there!"

Charlotte lunged as the cat sprang into the air and the chair tipped and a waterfall of blue dye cascaded out of the bucket and puddled on the dirt.

As she grabbed for the cat, her foot caught in the cord of the coffee urn. Puff yowled and went into attack mode, scratching Charlotte right through her rubber glove. Time stopped as the urn began to tip.

Charlotte imagined a tidal wave of water scalding the cat but seemed frozen into inaction.

Dawn did her own lunge and grabbed the urn just before it fell off the crate. Puff made her escape right through the lake of blue dye and Charlotte ripped off her glove. Three deep scratches were beading blood.

There was a moment of silence with only the sound of blue dye dripping.

"So. That was groovy fun," said Dawn, which somehow struck Charlotte as the funniest thing ever and they both fell into laughing.

"Okay. Stop. Stop!" said Charlotte with a final nose-dripping snort.

Still giggling, they bandaided Charlotte's hand and got reorganized.

"So," said Charlotte. "No blue. No green."

"It's okay. We've got red, yellow and orange. It'll still be good."

"Remember when we had our colors done that time at the mall? We'll both be autumn for the be-in."

They tied and dyed and dried. Blue-pawed Puff snuck back. The rubber gloves leaked. Charlotte wiggled her orange fingers at Dawn.

"What's this color? It's just like ... oh, come on, it's on the tip of my brain."

"Kwik-Tan! Remember Mandy North and the Summer Bronze Kwik-Tan and how her legs went orange?"

Charlotte nodded. "That's it."

Who else in the world would know about Mandy's leg disaster? Well, presumably Mandy, but her family moved to the States the next year.

"Where did they move to? Idaho?"

"Maybe. Or Iowa or Ohio. One of those ones."

"Somewhere where nobody knew about the shame of her orange legs and she could be a different person."

Charlotte stirred the dye. "If you moved away and you could be a different kind of person who would you be?"

"A person with straight hair. Folksinger-straight hair. So nobody would say, 'Hey, Dawn, what did you do to your hair?' You?"

"I'd be sophisticated, like a reporter on TV. They get to be really smart."

"You're already really smart."

Good old Dawn. She knew the right thing to say. Charlotte held up her bandaided Kwik-Tan hands.

"But not exactly sophisticated."

Dawn fished a bright red lump of bound-up fabric out of the bucket. "Is this done?"

"I think so. Moment of truth."

They snapped off the elastic bands and shook the fabric out into the air.

"Beautiful!"

"Beautiful-weird!"

"Like a sunset!"

"Like a sunset in a kaleidoscope!"
"So human," said Dawn.
"So be-in," said Charlotte.

Three

Charlotte was doodling. Martian flowers bloomed in the margins of her notebook.

Would school be cooler if classes were called learn-ins?

In the last year of elementary school on the last class of the last day before spring break, adding "in" didn't work. It was Charlotte's favorite subject, English, with her favorite teacher of all time, Miss O.O. McGough, but today the hour was dragging. In fact, the whole week had felt stretched out, just delaying holidays and especially the be-in.

Straight-A Sylvia was standing at the front of the class talking about *The Lord of the Rings, Volume Three: The Return of the King. The Lord of the Rings* was not on the curriculum, of course, but O.O. had thrown the curriculum out the window. Students got to read whatever they wanted. It was O.O.'s last year of teaching before retirement, and she had decided to "go rogue."

First thing in September she told the class that everyone was going to get a B in English.

"All you have to do is read. You are required to keep a list and once in a while you have to tell the class what you're reading and one interesting thing about it, but no book reports are required or indeed permitted. No book reports, no exams, no projects. Just reading and a bit of talking. We'll devote the last hour of every day to this plan. I do not have permission to do this but I've wanted to try it for my whole teaching career and what can they do to me now? Fire me? I am invincible."

At this point in the speech O.O. had assumed a superhero pose, which looked especially goofy as she was less than five feet tall and skinny as a kid.

"You still have to have marks so everyone is getting a B and we can stop thinking about that from this moment to the last syllable of recorded time."

This plan did not go over well with Sylvia Lane, Straight-A Queen. "Can we do extra work and get an A?"

O.O. shook her head and smiled. "No. Bs all around."

Sylvia may have objected but the guys in the back row liked it. They punched and nudged Larry into asking questions.

"What do we gotta read?"

"Absolutely anything," said O.O. "I'm going to bring in my entire book collection. You can borrow anything and if you want to keep the book you can. I'm clearing out. Or you can bring in a book from the library or from home."

Punch, punch, kick, kick. "Can it be like a comic or a magazine?"

"Magazine" was obviously code for *Playboy* but O.O. just nodded.

"Print of any sort. Follow your passions. Snicker away, Neil Cameron. Unlikely as this seems now when you are an unappetizing lump of unevolved dough, you are going to grow up to be a perfectly splendid human being and when you do, you will look back on grade seven and remember me and find that I am right."

The other person who seemed uneasy about the plan was Dorcas Radger. She asked O.O. if she could read the Bible. O.O. said of course she could and that the Bible was a rich work of literature.

Dorcas made Charlotte uncomfortable. She knew she should feel sorry for her because of her awful mother. Mrs. Radger was a member of city council and her thing was cleaning up the city. Not litter, but "moral filth." The summer before grade seven she had walked up and down the nude beach out near the university with a sign saying *Clothe Thy Nakedness*. There were pictures in the paper.

But there was also something kind of scary about Dorcas. Snobby and scary, like she was just getting ready to be mean.

Usually the hour was pretty fun. Somebody would say what they'd been reading and maybe read a few sentences aloud and then the class would talk about it. If it was a story or a poem O.O. would say something about the words or the characters. If it was a book about something or someone, the class talked about that something or someone. Over the year they'd discussed how people are manipulated by advertising and are ghosts real and who really killed President Kennedy.

Two people had read the same book all year. Larry read *The Guinness Book of World Records* and Dorcas read the Bible. None of the back-row snickerers had actually turned up with *Playboy*.

O.O. had lots of books about teenagers and Charlotte had gulped down most of them. The kids in those books all had big problems like mental illness, handicaps, pregnancy and being in gangs. But then Charlotte discovered *Pride and Prejudice* and she got stuck on it, starting again at the beginning as soon as she finished it. She'd reported on it three times because there was so much to say.

Usually the last hour was a good hour but *The Lord of the Rings* wasn't holding Charlotte's attention that Thursday. The back-row boys were restless, too.

Sylvia was bragging about how many pages there were in all three volumes of the trilogy (she had not given up on her hopes of inflating a B) when the door burst open, banging against the wall.

Sylvia dropped *The Return of the King*. An arm appeared. Attached to the arm was Mrs. Radger. She was holding a copy of *Catcher in the Rye* at arm's length, like you would hold a used diaper.

Catcher in the Rye had gone around the room like wildfire earlier in the year after Peter Lindos read a sexy bit out loud, probably on a dare from Larry. Charlotte had given it a try but she just didn't like that boy, Holden. He seemed like a spoiled rich kid. And the sexy bits were actually kind of upsetting.

Stump, stump, stump. Mrs. Radger walked across the front of the room to stand by O.O.'s desk. Sylvia stepped back against the blackboard.

"Is this filth your book?" Mrs. Radger had a booming voice.

Charlotte glanced over at Dorcas, who went from pale to paler.

"I don't know if it's my copy," said O.O. "Look at the flyleaf and see if my name is in it. And, by the way, have you signed in at the office? Parents are always welcome in the class but all visitors need to sign in."

"Sign in. Pah!"

Pah. It was like air released from a balloon.

"Have you actually *read* this book?" Mrs. Radger was getting pinker and pinker.

O.O. nodded. "Yes, I try to keep up with what my students are reading. Have *you* read it, Mrs. Radger?"

"Read it? This smut? I have no need to read it, thank you very much. I have read all I need to know about this so-called novel." Mrs. Radger made the words "smut" and "novel" sound worse than the worst words in *Catcher in the Rye.*

O.O. pushed her chair back and started to stand but Mrs. Radger stepped farther into the room and O.O. froze.

She approached O.O.'s desk and held up the open book with both hands.

"There's only one thing to do with this muck."

With a grunt, she tried to rip the book in half. But it wasn't that easy to tear a hardcover book in half. She tried a couple of times and the back row started to giggle. Her pink face darkened and she gave a magenta glare in their general direction and then heaved the book into the metal wastepaper basket.

Clang!

"You will be hearing more about this," she said and turned to go. Then she stuck out her hand and commanded, "Dorcas. Come."

Nobody giggled then. Charlotte glanced sideways and caught Dawn's eye. There was a whole conversation in her raised eyebrows.

The door slammed behind the whirlwind.

O.O. pulled the book out of the garbage can. She riffled through the pages. They were blacked out, big chunks of black. She seemed kind of stunned.

"Yes. My copy. I wish Dorcas had spoken to me about this."

Sylvia picked up the 512 pages of *Return of the King* and slid back to her desk.

Then the bell rang.

The usual rumble started and O.O.'s vagueness disappeared.

"Sit!" She sounded like a fierce dog-training lady.

"Right. Here's what's going to happen now. Nobody from this class is going to talk about this. Nobody is going to tease Dorcas when she comes back to school. We're not going to turn it into a joke. If someone starts doing this, it's your responsibility to shut them up. That must have been horribly embarrassing for Dorcas. We're not our parents and we're not responsible for them. We've talked a lot about censorship this year. The freedom to read what you want is important. Kindness is even more important. When you get back after holidays we'll have a new copy of Salinger in our class library. And nobody will have been humiliated. Is that clear?"

Mumble. Mumble. Shrug. Shrug. There was the roar of students passing in the hall.

"I need an answer. Is. That. Clear?" O.O. looked like she was facing down an attack dog.

There were nods all over the room.

"Right. You're good people. Off you go. Happy holidays. Read up a storm."

Charlotte glanced back at O.O. as she left. The teacher was sitting at her desk, looking out the window. The back of her head and her shoulders looked old.

FOUR

Friday and Saturday were delicious. Sleeping in, eating breakfast at noon, watching *People in Conflict* on TV, hanging out while Claude made cinnamon buns, taking said buns down to Green Thumb and lounging around with Miss Biscuit who did the Saturday shift at the shop, playing the radio loud when everyone was out of the house, reliving the Mrs. Radger drama with Dawn on the phone ("Did you notice that little bits of spit came out of her mouth?") until Dad came by and tapped his watch.

But Sunday, Be-In Day, Dawn phoned early to report a crisis.

"Charlotte! Phone!" Claude's voice broke into her dreams. She stumbled down to the front hall.

"They've been reading the paper and now they're all worried about marijuana and a 'police presence.'"

Mr. and Mrs. Novak were hard to figure out. In some ways they were way cooler than the Quintans, with their interior decoration and all that. But they were also stricter. More "old country," as Dawn put it. Dawn had been born in the old country but she was only interested in being one hundred percent Canadian.

She was furious. "They're going to drive us!"

"Is that so bad?" Charlotte stretched around the corner of the hall to look out the window. "It looks kind of rainy."

"Charlotte! It's going to be SO embarrassing to be dropped off, like our first day at kindergarten. They just treat me like a child. Can you come over?"

"Uhh, sure. I'll bring all the stuff."

By the time Charlotte arrived at the Novaks', Dawn had bounced back from furious. Mrs. Novak was wandering around in elegant loungewear with a cup of coffee, and Mr. Novak was nowhere to be seen.

There was an ironing board set up in the living room and the tie-dyes were festooned across the furniture.

The skirt looked great on the armchair.

"Try it on," said Mrs. Novak. "I want to see this hippies look."

Charlotte pulled on the skirt. Then she went into the hall to look in the full-length mirror.

She wanted to cry. She looked ridiculous. Like one of the younger, rounder children in *The Sound of Music*.

She couldn't go out in the world looking like this. Maybe she could just stay in her jeans. Maybe she wouldn't go to the be-in after all. What had made her agree to this whole thing?

Mrs. Novak walked by and turned Charlotte to face her.

"Oh, no, no, no. Take it off. Daliborka! Get the sewing machine!"

"Mo-om. *Dawn.*"

Dawn had turned up at kindergarten and announced her name as Dawn. Her parents sometimes forgot.

With much tsk-ing over the poor quality of the original workmanship, Mrs. Novak measured and pinned, cut and sewed, added elastic and darts, all at top speed and accompanied by the tinkling of small bells.

A final snip of threads and the skirt was ready. Held up in the air it looked basically the same, and Charlotte didn't hold out much hope. But Mrs. Novak had performed magic. Once on, it looked folky, not lumpy at all. And perfect with Dawn's peasant blouse.

Mrs. Novak gave an approving nod. "Good now."

"Leave up the ironing board," said Dawn. "I want you to iron my hair."

"Why would you do that? Your hair is fabulous."

"But does it go with a tie-dyed Laura Ashley dress? It does not."

"I think it goes."

"Joan Baez. Straight hair. Judy Collins. Straight hair. I rest my case."

"Bob Dylan has curly hair."

"Oh, good grief. Bob Dylan also has a beard."

Charlotte turned the iron to the lowest setting and took a deep breath. Dawn laid her head on the board and Charlotte pulled out a corkscrew curl and pressed it straight. It was very satisfying.

"It kind of smells like an animal. Come to think of it, I guess it *is* an animal."

The front door opened and closed and Mr. Novak stuck his head into the room. Charlotte didn't understand what Mr. Novak did for work but it involved night shifts.

"What is this about?"

"Canadian thing," said Dawn from underneath her curtain-straight hair. Over the years Charlotte had noticed that Dawn used "It's Canadian" as a reason to get away with a lot. It was the opposite of "old country."

It was nearly time to leave. Charlotte checked her bag, James's old backpack. Blanket, brush, cookies, hat, Coke and the chocolate Easter chicken that had appeared on the end of her bed that morning.

"Cevapcici?" said Mrs. Novak holding out a Tupperware container.

"Mo–om!" Dawn's voice sounded suspiciously un-Unteen. "Nobody takes meatballs to a be-in."

Charlotte took one last look in the mirror. "Are sandals really the right thing? It might be wet."

"Nothing else really works with this look. We can put up with wet feet."

The falling mist started as the Novak car pulled out of the parking garage.

"Oh, heck. Look. My hair is just curling right back up. I *am* going to look like Bob Dylan."

"Well, minus the beard."

By the time they reached Second Beach the mist had gained confidence and Mr. Novak had turned on the windshield wipers. Blur. View. Blur. View.

The big open field between the road and the ocean was ringed with trees.

A band was standing on the back of a truck — the kind of truck that went in parades. There was a huge crowd. The sound carried across the field, through the trees, up the slope and into the closed car.

Dawn rolled down her window. "This is fine. We can just get out here."

"Yes, stop here," said Mrs. Novak. "Don't shame the girls."

Dawn exhaled loudly and Charlotte gave her a grin. The only thing more embarrassing than being dropped off at the be-in by your parents was one of your parents figuring out that you were embarrassed.

Mr. Novak pulled over. A couple of boys with long flowing hair slid by the car carrying boards covered in earrings.

"What is this about?" asked Mr. Novak. "Scruffing boys with jewelry?"

"Scruffy," said Dawn, "And it's not about anything. It's just beads."

"Pretty," said Mrs. Novak. "Hippie fashion."

"Don't say hippie," said Dawn.

"Wrong word?"

"No, it's the right word but … it's corny."

"Corny?"

Dawn pushed open the back door of the car. "We're going."

"Umbrella?" said Mrs. Novak.

"*Nobody* goes to the be-in with an umbrella," said Dawn. "We'll find a tree or something."

"Five o'clock," said Mr. Novak. "Right here. Remember. No psychedelics."

The big blue Plymouth pulled away slowly. Mrs. Novak waved. Charlotte had the odd impression that she was sorry to leave.

Dawn rolled her eyes. "How can he know the word psychedelic when he doesn't even know the word scruffy?"

They stood at the top of a little rise by the side of the road. There were blankets and tarps, colors muted by the fine rain. The edges of the field were slick with grass but the main part was sticky with mud.

Charlotte remembered a preschool visit to a farm. She had expected a life-sized version of her play farm, all neat fences and plump animals. Instead it was dirty and smelly, the fields all churned up with mud from cows' hoofs. The funny thing was, when the class got back to preschool they all painted pictures of the farm but nobody painted mud. Everybody painted the play farm.

There was a loud electric squawk from the stage.

Dawn raised her eyebrows. "Let's go."

If she could have, Charlotte would have bailed. She hitched her pack more securely on her back and took a deep breath.

Only six hours to go. Only six hours to Be.

They picked their way down the slope, trying not to slip on the wet grass, holding the tie-dye skirts out of the mud. Three boys with Beatles hair were on the stage. Their band had guitars and some horns, a golden drum set and huge amplifiers covered in plastic. The sound rolled across the field.

Charlotte didn't recognize the song. In fact, it didn't really seem like a song at all. More like the noise of a storm. She wondered what the seagulls thought. They were used to being the loudest things around but they could not compete.

People sat on blankets and tarps on the ground, and around the edges people danced. Charlotte spied a patch of grass at the edge of the crowd. It wasn't too muddy. "Let's stop here."

"This is way too far away," said Dawn. "We'll hardly hear the band."

Charlotte thought they could probably have heard the band clear across English Bay, but she was trying to be as brave as Dawn so she followed her right into the middle of the dancing, singing, smoking, drinking, bubble-blowing, kite-flying, laughing crowd.

A girl who looked like Juliet in velvet and lace, except for the hiking boots, motioned to her.

"Come sit."

Charlotte glanced at Dawn who gave a little nod.

Charlotte took out the blanket and they put it down on the edge of Juliet's tarp.

"Thank you," said Dawn. "Great spot."

Juliet reached into a large tapestry bag (so much prettier

than James's khaki backpack) and brought out two apples. She held them out, one balanced on each upturned palm.

"Fruit," she said. "A gift."

She had weird eyes, starey, like doll eyes.

"Um, thanks," said Charlotte. Did Juliet think that they didn't know that apples were fruit? She couldn't look at Dawn.

Dawn was being nicer. "Fruit. Yeah. Cool."

Juliet then floated up and dissolved away into the crowd.

Charlotte pointed at the apple. "Fruit," she said in a deep important voice.

"Don't be like that," said Dawn.

"What like that?"

"You know. Superior."

"Come on, Dawn, she's a nutbar."

"Look. We're at a be-in, right? We're just supposed to *be*. You're always judging."

Judging? Always? A nutbar was a nutbar. Where was this coming from? The distance between them on the blanket suddenly seemed like a city block. Charlotte pulled her feet in and hugged her knees. When Dawn got in this mood there was no discussing it. She would maintain her position to the death. To save the day somebody needed to patch over the crack. And it wasn't going to be Dawn doing the patching.

"You're right. She was nice with the apples. Seeing as how we brought nothing but junk to eat."

Dawn accepted the patch. "Yeah. We could have had meatballs, of course."

41

The rain let up and Charlotte leaned back against her elbows and watched the passing parade.

Dawn had said that it was all about the clothes, but really it seemed to be all about hair. Who knew there were so many kinds? Long, every variety of curly, straight, wild, fluffy, braided, greasy, pulled back (boys in ponytails!), piled up, swirling around as everyone danced. And all the colors. Charlotte thought of horses. Bay, roan, chestnut, palomino, tortoiseshell.

Tortoiseshell? No. That was cats. Or, come to think of it, tortoises.

Dawn was obviously also thinking about hair. "Look at all the beards."

"Isn't it weird how some match head-hair and some don't? It must be fun to grow a beard or a moustache. Just to see."

"I wouldn't have one of those big lumberjack ones, though. Things could nest in there. Yuck. I'd have a neat one."

An especially long weedy beard walked by.

"How long can they grow if they never cut them?"

"Maybe as long as head hair?"

"It's like you can turn your face into a work of art."

"Nice for guys, cause otherwise they don't get to be fancy much."

A new band jumped on the stage truck and their rhythms were dancier. Charlotte was just about to suggest to Dawn that they join the crowd of jumping, jiggling, waving dancers when a boy (man?) grabbed her hand, and then Dawn's.

"Come on!"

His hand was sand-papery and callused like Uncle Claude's, but not very clean. Charlotte peered around him at Dawn who raised her eyebrows and grinned. The guy had long ginger-colored hair and a ginger beard just one shade darker. He was wearing burnt-orange-colored pants and shirt. Run, run as fast as you can. You can't catch me. I'm the gingerbread man.

It was crazy-wild dancing. Charlotte thought of school dances in the gym. One of the horrible things was that you'd be standing talking to a friend and some boy would come over and ask one of you to dance. It was just as awful if you were the asked or the not-asked. If you were the not-asked you'd feel left out but it was actually worse if you were the asked because then you'd feel like you were abandoning your friend. It was one of the many dilemmas that had driven Charlotte to her Unteen position.

But here it was totally different. Gingerbread Boy just held out two hands and asked both Charlotte *and* Dawn.

It was completely unlike a school dance. There were no partners. Someone would meet your eye and you would dance with them for a second or a minute, or you would just dance by yourself. Gingerbread Boy was folded into the crowd almost immediately and Charlotte soon lost track of Dawn. It didn't matter. The booming music came in through her pores and it was like the dance was a random but beautiful pattern they were all making up together — a pattern without rules.

When the song ended with a loud squawk, Charlotte looked down and the entire hem of her skirt was muddy.

Her sandals and feet were slick with dirt. As she headed back to the blanket her feet started to slip around in her sandals so she took them off and went barefoot. Barefoot in mud, her feet felt like they were four years old.

When she got back to the blanket there was no sign of Dawn. But Juliet was there. She was dancing to the music while sitting down, flipping her hair back and forth and smiling a faraway smile. Charlotte reminded herself not to be judgy and actually, sitting with her was very comfortable, like sitting with a dog, no conversation required. Every so often Juliet would comment.

"Wow."

"Far out."

"It blows your mind."

Charlotte noticed some police on horseback standing at the edge of the field. She and Dawn had often visited the police stables at the entrance to the park. She knew some of the horses by name.

"Hey, wanna go see the horses?"

Juliet scowled. "But, those are the cops!"

"And …"

"The *fuzz*. Look at them. They're here to shut down the be-in. Pigs."

"They're not that kind of police."

Charlotte had seen the TV news where bad police beat up protestors and all that. But that wasn't here.

"Hmph," said Juliet, and she went back to dancing with her hair.

Charlotte looked out over the bobbing heads, through music that was so loud that you could almost see it, to the gray beach and the grayer ocean beyond.

Hippies! They had figured out how to be the ultimate Unteens. They weren't kids. They were adult in size and they were smoking and making out. (Seriously! It seemed rude to look but really, she'd never seen kissing like that in public. Well, not in private either, come to think of it.) But they were also just playing, doing goofy dances, laughing, wearing costumes, getting muddy, blowing bubbles, not worrying about manners and being on time.

Like children. Flower children.

Maybe there was a way to be that wasn't either kid or adult but a different thing altogether. A third choice that wasn't teen.

Charlotte didn't really want to be a hippie. Already her dirty feet were getting itchy and she wanted to be able to pet the police horses.

But the third-choice idea. It was a new thought and it was like ginger ale for the brain. It made her feel like she could fly or do a perfect front flip or walk on her hands.

At that moment Dawn came back. She was with a boy who was just about as opposite from the be-in as you could imagine, a kind of anti-matter of hippie. He had very short tidy hair shaved up the sides of his head, and he was dressed in crisp jeans and a white T-shirt. He was so clean that he seemed to have a little halo around him.

How was he staying so clean?

The second he arrived at the blanket, the sun peeped out.

"This is Tom Ed," said Dawn. "He's from Texas. He's a draft dodger."

Later, when Charlotte saw those T-shirts that declared *Today is the first day of the rest of your life,* she thought of that moment.

The damp blanket, her muddy toes, the music in her pores, the hippie-sweet air and the tall, bright-faced Texan.

FiVE

"You can come stay at our house."

Tom Ed had been describing where he was "crashing," and the invitation just popped out of Charlotte's mouth.

Tom Ed gave a slow smile. "How will your folks feel about that?"

Folks. That would be parents. Charlotte was doing translation. She was used to accents from New Canadian kids at school but she'd never heard Texan before. It was sort of slow and wide. Relaxing.

"It'll be fine. We've always got people staying."

"Yeah," said Dawn. "They've got Uncle Claude who's there half the time and there was Lena from up north taking that nursing course and those little kids."

"Frankie and Susie. Their parents were having a divorce. And that Czech refugee guy whose mean landlord beat him up. But we've never had a draft dodger. There's lots of talk about draft dodgers at Meeting."

"Meeting?" said Tom Ed.

"Quaker Meeting. We're Quakers."

"Ah!" said Tom Ed. "I know about Quakers. Never met any, though, till this moment."

Tom Ed had a way of listening that was extra alert, listening with psychedelic ears, angling his head like a budgie.

Charlotte thought about the boys she knew — at school, at Meeting, James and his friends. Canadian boys didn't do that budgie thing. They kept their heads screwed on tight to their necks.

The conversation meandered all over the place. Dawn talked about a dream she had where her bicycle melted. Juliet, whose name was actually Janice, began to talk in full sentences about her aquarium and her allergy to pineapple and how e.e. cummings was her favorite poet.

Tom Ed told them the basics. He was nineteen, from a town called Levelland, and had two brothers and one sister. But mostly he asked questions.

"What astrological sign are y'all?"

"Charlotte and me are both Aquarius," said Dawn. "It's the best because we have our own song."

"Cool!" said Juliet and began to sing about the dawning of the age of Aquarius, mystic crystal revelation and all.

Tom Ed was intrigued by tie-dye. "I don't recall seeing that in Levelland. Is it Canadian?"

The truth was, the tie-dye had been a big mistake. All the other girls wore either jeans and leather vests or lace and velvet like Janice. Charlotte hadn't said anything because it had been Dawn's idea. But she was glad when her skirt got toned down with mud and she was relieved she wasn't the one in the all-over tie-dyed dress.

"No," said Dawn. "It's not Canadian. It's ..." She looked at Charlotte.

"Groovy?"

Groovy set them off on a round of giggles. Then Tom Ed had to hear the whole story of blue-pawed Puff.

"At least we haven't seen anyone from school," said Dawn. "We look kind of ridiculous."

"Yeah," said Charlotte. "Like practice targets."

"It did cross my mind that it was good that Canadians aren't partial to guns," said Tom Ed. Charlotte and Dawn both punched him in the shoulder.

The afternoon disappeared as they let the music boom through them. They danced a bit, sang along, making up the words when they didn't know them, which was mostly. They ate all the snacks.

Finally, Janice rolled up her tarp and before she started to float away into the crowd she made the peace sign to them and they all peace-signed back.

Then it was five o'clock and Mr. Novak was waiting in the blue Plymouth.

Peace, love and grooviness got a bit battered on the way home. As soon as Mr. Novak heard that Tom Ed was a draft dodger he immediately started talking, in a pointed way, about his time in the Yugoslav People's Army.

It always amazed Charlotte how adults could get away with being rude. It was one of the things that nobody seemed to notice. Nobody except Jane Austen. That's what was so great about *Pride and Prejudice*. Jane Austen noticed. If Charlotte had been Elizabeth Bennet she would have thought of something perfect to say, but she wasn't, so she just sat in the back seat beside Tom Ed and felt grumpy on his behalf.

Tom Ed seemed to take care of himself though. He addressed Mr. Novak as "sir" and was more polite than Charlotte had ever seen a teenage boy be.

Mr. Novak unbent a tiny bit. It probably helped that Tom Ed wasn't the least bit scruffing.

When the Novaks stopped at Charlotte's house, Dawn gave Charlotte a look that had a whole conversation in it. It was something like, "Oh, you're so lucky. Your very own draft dodger! And now you get to have dinner with him while I have to go home and have Easter dinner with my aunt and uncle and my drippy cousins and I'm so *jealous*! But I know you'll phone me later and tell me every tiny little detail."

Charlotte's half of the conversation was contained in a nod.

{l}

Charlotte took Tom Ed around to the kitchen door.

"We don't use the front door because it's hard to get through the front hall with all the plants. It's the brightest room so it's good for them. James calls it the intensive care ward."

"James?"

"My brother."

50

The kitchen was full of steam and sizzle. Uncle Claude was making a racket with frying pans.

Charlotte did the introductions and Claude shook hands with Tom Ed without taking off his oven mitts.

"Well, frost my socks. A genuine American draft dodger. I've read about you fellas."

"Pleased to meet you, sir. What's that you're fixin?"

Somehow Claude knew what "fixin" meant.

"Stir-fried vegetables. It's a Chinese thing. I like to do it for Miss Biscuit. They were missionaries over there somewhere, weren't they? Once upon a time? It ought to make them feel right at home. I figured it would jazz up the Easter ham. Lots of work, though. Everything's cut up into small pieces. I don't think the guys at the camp are going to go for it."

Charlotte waved away some of the smoke. "Is it burning?"

"You have to get the oil smoking hot. Set the table, would you?"

"How many?"

"Basic five plus Miss Biscuit plus our new guest."

"So, eight."

"Isn't that seven?" asked Tom Ed.

Actually he said, "Idn't that seb'm?" but Charlotte was already fluent in Texan and jumped in to explain.

"Miss Biscuit is actually two people. There's Enid Biscuit and her younger-by-one-year sister Ethel. But we always just say Miss Biscuit."

"Family?"

"No. Quaker friends and they work in the store."

Charlotte was bumping the cutlery drawer shut with her hip when Tom Ed took the knives and forks out of her hands.

"Dining room this way?"

{l}

Under the dining-room table Charlotte's newly washed toes stretched out in clean socks. A long afternoon of rain and dancing and too much Coke and she was floating. She found herself staring at Tom Ed's hands. They were large and bony.

You could tell a lot about a person by the way they ate. For example, it was obvious that the Dodger was American. He ate like the Quaker Elder from Boston who stayed with them last year.

Tom Ed cut a piece of meat, laid his knife along the side of his plate, transferred his fork to his right hand, stabbed the meat and some vegetables with his fork and then ate it. Then he transferred his fork to his left hand and started again. It seemed complicated but it also had a rhythm to it.

"Do you have any brothers and sisters, Tom Ed?" Miss Biscuit always liked to get people's families sorted out.

"Yes, ma'am. I have an older brother JJ, an older sister Jimilene and there's the little one, Randy."

Mid-dinner the conversation turned to the Vietnam War. People talked about the war at Meeting and Charlotte knew about the marches and the protests, but it always seemed like something that happened in another country and on TV.

Tom Ed sitting at the table scooping up scalloped potatoes made it more real.

"What is your position on war resistance?" Dad leaned across his plate and addressed Tom Ed.

Tom Ed put down his fork, swallowed and wiped his mouth.

"I know you're Quakers but I have to say that I'm not a pacifist. I hope that's not disrespectful."

"Not disrespectful at all," said Dad. "Tell us more."

"But please feel free to keep eating," said Mom. "Paul has a habit of going into interrogation mode just when one is chewing."

"I'm not a pacifist because I think there are necessary wars. I would have gone to war against Hitler. But this war doesn't make sense. It was a mistake from the beginning and now we can't get out because we're not allowed to be seen to lose. Nixon and his 'peace with honor.' Ffffft! I'm not going to go and be killed, or even worse, kill other people just so that some guy in the schoolyard can save face."

Miss Biscuit nodded vigorously.

"It's the old story."

"Boys on the playground."

Up to this point James had been quiet but he set down his water glass and leaned across the table.

"If you avoid the draft by coming up here to Canada doesn't it mean that somebody else has to go in your place? Probably some guy who can't get out of it? Like some poor kid?"

Charlotte waited for Mom to say, "Now, James," because it sounded borderline rude but everyone just waited for Tom Ed to answer.

He abandoned his fork once again. "Yes, it likely does mean that but I can't go over there in the name of a war that is at best unjustified and at worst immoral. Some of the things that Americans are doing over there …" Tom Ed swallowed hard.

"Where do you get your information?" James wasn't letting it go.

"Look. I know stuff, okay? There's no real good choice here. Only bad and worse. I chose bad."

He gave James a hard look and Charlotte smelled a whiff of the playground and thanked her lucky stars, for about the millionth time, that she wasn't a boy.

Miss Biscuit jumped in. "We really admire you young people standing up for what you believe in. Change has to come from the grass roots. Do your parents support you?"

Tom Ed put down his fork again. "No, ma'am."

"Such a shame. We know what that's like, don't we, Enid? We were members of the WSPU when we were girls. Father was just livid. He threatened to lock us out of the house."

"WSPU?" said Tom Ed.

"Women's Social and Political Union."

"Suffragettes."

"Did you go on protest marches?" said Tom Ed.

"At first. But the motto was 'Deeds, Not Words.'"

"What kind of deeds?"

Charlotte expected that Miss Biscuit would say something like singing protest songs or maybe blocking traffic or something. (Did they even have traffic when they were girls?)

"It started with breaking shop windows. Then it went on to bombing stately homes."

"Frost my socks!" said Uncle Claude. "You were setting bombs?"

Charlotte looked at Miss Biscuit. The sisters suddenly transformed from two old ladies into a pair of criminals.

"Well, not us personally. We were only seventeen and sixteen after all, and then the war came and it all rather fizzled for a while. But we went to the rallies and we approved, didn't we, Ethel? We wore our badges. They were portraits of Emmeline Pankhurst. They came with ribbons. Purple for …"

"… the royal blood that flows in the veins of every suffragette."

"Green for hope."

"And white for purity in private and public life."

"Doesn't sound that pure, bombing people's houses," said James.

"We didn't call them bombs, did we, Ethel? We just referred to them as things that blew up the mail."

"And they made sure nobody was in the houses at the time. Mrs. Pankhurst was very stern about that. Property, not loss of life."

"Point is, we understand about trying to change the minds of those in power. Without the vote, civil disobedience was really the only option."

"Father *did* lock us out, remember, Enid? Well, he tried to, but Cook just let us in the area door. Cook was a secret suffragette. Father was terrified that we would make a spectacle of ourselves in public. 'I don't want a daughter of mine with her picture in the morning papers.'"

Tom Ed wiped his mouth again. "Yes, ma'am. Same with my daddy. He worries what everybody in town will think. He probably worries as much about that as about patriotism and serving your country."

Daddy! Who called their father Daddy after about age five? Charlotte saw James make a face.

Over pie, the conversation moved on to another war — the squirrels in the attic of Miss Biscuit's house.

"They seem to be eating the wires. We had to have a man in."

"We felt terrible. There were new babies."

"But it can't have been good for them, eating wires."

"He trapped them all in a cage and he's going to take them to Stanley Park and release them."

Tom Ed frowned. "Why didn'e just shoot 'em?"

Miss Biscuit stopped mid-chew. "Well, I don't believe the pest control people are issued with guns."

"If anybody had trouble with squirrels or other pests in our town they just got Duane to come. He had an air-pump pellet rifle. He was a sharp shooter for a kid."

This time Mom stopped eating. "How much of a kid?"

"Around twelve."

"A twelve-year-old with a gun?"

"Well, yes, ma'am. But he was good. He practiced on rats."

Eating ground to a halt. Charlotte felt it was her turn to prompt Tom Ed to continue.

"Where did he get the rats?"

"Well," said Tom Ed, "this is where I come into the story. Duane would pay five cents a live rat to any kid. We had a good source of rats. At the end of our block there was a big vacant lot filled with construction garbage — plywood, sheet metal, stuff like that. Good for building stuff and collecting stuff. We'd go down there with empty milk cartons, one end opened up. Then one kid would pull up something plywood or metal and usually a rat would run out. Then we'd run and step on the rat and scoop up the head into the open carton, then lift up our foot and turn the carton upright real quick and close it up. Then deliver the rat to Duane and get our nickel. It took some skill."

"I almost hate to ask this," said Dad, "but exactly what did Duane do with the rats?"

"He'd get somebody to let them go and then he'd shoot at 'em."

"With his gun?" said Mom faintly.

"Yes, ma'am, that's right."

{I}

Dawn phoned after dinner.

"So? Is he going to stay at your place?"

"Uh-huh."

"Oh, boy, you're *so* lucky. Your own draft dodger. For how long?"

"Hmmm, not sure."

Conversations at the Quintan house often involved being a woman of few words. The phone was in the front hall by the stairs, right in the middle of everything. Charlotte noticed that when you flipped through the phone book sometimes you saw, under the first number, another number that said "Children's Phone." Who *were* those lucky people?

This was not a teenager complaint. It was a human-being complaint.

"He absolutely can't leave until I get back from music camp. Why do I even have to *go* to music camp? Maybe I just won't go. Maybe I'll get sick, but just until the bus leaves tomorrow morning. Oh, that won't work. I'm doomed. Look, you'll just have to remember every single thing that happens between now and Saturday."

Charlotte spiraled the phone cord around her finger. Dad walked by.

"Charlotte, quit messing up the cord. I just fixed it."

The phone cord was one of Dad's special interests. He felt that if the phone cord was tidy, there was hope for cosmic order.

"Charlotte! Promise?"

"Uh-huh."

"Promise squared?"

"Uh-huh."

"Promise to the nth power?"

"*Yes!*"

"Okay. Call me before I leave tomorrow."

"Before eight?"

"Come on, Charlotte. It's only fair. Plus, I was the one who found him in the first place."

She had a point. "Okay."

SiX

Monday morning and no school. Was there a more delicious combination? Charlotte stretched out and tipped Puff off the edge of the bed. It wasn't like the Easter holidays were going to be glamorous. Some kids from her class were going on trips. Sylvia Lane's family was off to the cottage.

But Charlotte's plans were more modest. Sleeping in, going shopping with Monique, playing some badminton with Donna, a couple of evenings of babysitting and a feast of daytime TV. Five days in a row of *People in Conflict*.

Life was good.

At seven Charlotte had rolled out of bed to phone Dawn as promised. She reassured her that she wouldn't let the Dodger leave (as if she had control over that) and she said goodbye, all without actually waking up, so she was able to roll right back into bed for another delicious three hours.

She gave another stretch. The purring sound of the lawn mower wafted in the window. James?

She looked out the window. Tom Ed! The lawn looked very precise.

Shrugging on some beat-up clothes, she wandered outside, grabbing a banana on the way, and met Tom Ed coming up the back stretch.

He gave a huge smile. "Howdy, Miz Charlotte."

Movie-star teeth.

Charlotte felt like she could say anything. "How come Americans have such good teeth?"

"I don't know about Americans in general but where I grew up there's a high concentration of fluoride in the water."

Charlotte felt a wave of easiness break over her. It had been a real question and Tom Ed was really answering it. He didn't seem to find the question cute. He was treating her like an Unteen.

"Nobody has cavities. Nobody goes to the dentist, except after they get old and they have to get all their teeth pulled and get false teeth."

"Really? You've never been to the dentist?"

"Nope."

No dentists. No needles, no drills, no spit in the sink.

"I want to rewind my life and grow up in Texas."

Tom Ed tipped up the mower, sat on the ground and started cleaning grass gunk off the blades with a stick. "Would you be the same person?"

"What?"

"Same family, different place. Would you be the same person?"

61

Charlotte sank down on the grass. Weird. This question —
how much can you change and still be you — was something
she had thought about for as far back as she could remember. What if she lived in the house next door? What if she
had different parents or grew up speaking Japanese or wearing
wooden shoes? What if she'd been born a boy? This was a reli-
able question for boring car trips or too-hot-to-sleep nights
but she had never thought to discuss it with someone else.

"I think so. If I had the same family I'd be me. Only better
teeth. You?"

"Not sure. But I think I'm about to find out. Will I be the
same person in Canada?"

Tom Ed gave the mower a wipe with a rag and pushed it
back to the shed door. Then he came and plunked himself
down beside Charlotte.

"Want half a banana?"

"Sure."

Charlotte gave him the half with the peel.

"Say, I've been wondering." Tom Ed pointed to the cherry
tree, pink with bloom. "What's that thing up there?"

"Just what's left of a treehouse. Dad built it. It used to have
a ladder and a window. Once Dawn and I slept there overnight. But bits have fallen off."

"Treehouse? I've never seen one."

"You didn't have a treehouse? But I thought you were
always building things."

"Yeah, but we didn't have any trees. We built forts."

"No trees?"

"Nope. 'Cept in parks. A few shrubby things in gardens sometimes, but no trees. Nothing to block the view."

"The view of what?"

"The view of what trees would have blocked, which was more and more of nothing as far as the eye can see. There's this thing they say in Lubbock. You can see clear to the next county and if you stand on a can of tuna you can see to Oklahoma. So I've never seen a treehouse and I've never been in a treehouse, which is a situation that is going to change right quick. Let's go up there."

"It's probably rotten by now, and the ladder's gone."

"So we'll climb."

Charlotte looked at the rough bark of the tree. It looked scratchy.

"Maybe I should get the stepladder."

"Naw. I'll just boost you up. I can climb up after you."

"How?"

"I'll show you. Come on."

When they reached the tree Tom Ed leaned over and laced his fingers together.

"Step here, and then step onto my shoulders, then a short step up to the front door of the house. Easy as stairs."

Why not? There was a bad moment between hands and shoulder when Charlotte bashed her knee into his ear. But Tom Ed didn't complain and she made it from shoulder to treehouse without further incident.

Tom Ed jumped up to grab a branch and then swung himself back and forth until he got his legs over it as well, and then pulled himself up. It was like a gymnastics thing.

"Not bad for a kid from no-tree-land, wouldn't you say?"

The tree had filled out since the treehouse was built, and the platform was now enclosed by black branches and pink flowers. Sunlight flickered on the grayed boards. It was even more like a bird's nest than Charlotte remembered. There was a small breeze.

"You can smell the water on the wind," said Tom Ed.

"What's that?"

"Where I come from it hardly ever rains, but when it does you can smell it coming. It's some sweet smell."

"I guess in Vancouver we smell that almost all the time so we don't notice it."

"Maybe so."

"It's nice of you to mow the lawn."

"Might as well make myself useful while I'm here. I'm going out today to look for work. One of the guys where I was crashing before? He gave me a lead."

"But nobody's going to be in their office today. It's Easter Monday."

"Easter Monday? Is that a holiday?"

"Well, yeah."

"Not in Texas. Easter's just Easter, on Sunday. It didn't tell me about that in the booklet."

"The booklet?"

"*Manual for Draft-Age Immigrants to Canada.* I've read it

three times. I'm going to become a real Canadian. I know about the French thing and the House of Commons and how Alberta's like Texas, but I didn't know about Easter Monday. So, no job-hunting today." He leaned back against the trunk of the tree.

"Charlotte: question. Are all Canadian families like yours?"

She thought of the dinner conversation, from bombs to squirrels. "You mean weird?"

"No, I mean kind."

"Um. I don't know. Are we that different from your family?"

"Man alive! You have no idea. You know how your daddy and mother ask your opinion on issues? They seem to actually want to know what you think. If my daddy asks us a question he's checking to make sure that we know the right answer. He's trying to get at us. Randy, the little guy? He's still kind of cute so he speaks up a bit, but that's going to be over real soon. I feel bad that I'm not there. Not that JJ was able to protect me. Daddy's always trying to make sure that he's in control. Over everything. Over Mother, too. Jimilene escaped, finally. Her husband seems like a decent guy. I don't think he's going to beat her up."

"Did your dad beat you up?"

"Well, he whipped me some."

"Whipped?"

"Yeah, with a belt."

Charlotte's stomach headed toward the treehouse floor. She knew there were families who were different from hers. She knew there were dads who were yellers, and mothers who got drunk and passed out. The Landry kids had a dad in jail. Sometimes at Dawn's house she could feel the air go gluey with the tension between Mr. and Mrs. Novak.

But … a belt? She didn't know anyone who got hit with a belt.

"Did he hit you all?"

Tom Ed shifted and the treehouse creaked. A few pink blossoms floated down.

"Well, JJ got a pass. JJ was the son Daddy wanted. Just like a ditto copy of himself. Tough-talking, football-playing, patriotic. He didn't argue. He didn't run away. He went there. He went to Nam."

"He was a soldier?"

"Yes. Couldn't wait. Wanted to go over there and save the world from the evils of Communism."

"I don't get the Communism thing. It just sounds like sharing to me, and being fair. Why is it evil?"

Tom Ed shook his head. "I wonder thát, too. It's all about Russians and spies and I don't know what-all. But JJ believed it all and he was hell-bent on going over to fight the guerrillas. When I first heard that I thought he was going over to fight gorillas, like the big apes. Well, it kind of made sense, jungle and all. And I was going to go, too. I always wanted to do what JJ did. I wanted to be just like him so that Dad would respect me. You know those stories with the older brother who does everything right? Slays the dragon, solves the riddle, wins the fortune —"

"Marries the princess?"

Tom Ed snorted. "Yeah, all that. Quarterback. Then there's the younger brother who messes up? That was me."

"Like the prodigal son?"

"Yeah. 'Cept Daddy's not going to be killing any fatted calf for me. Not that I'm going home anyway. Even if I wanted to."

"But you get to go home when the war ends, right?"

"Nope. The U.S. has never granted amnesty to draft evaders. I'm gone for good."

Tom Ed paused. Charlotte reached up and broke off a twig of blossoms.

To never go home? What if that was her? She wanted to go all over the world and see the Taj Mahal and the Eiffel Tower and kangaroos, but she would always want to come back to Vancouver.

Tom Ed hadn't just crossed the border. He had left his whole life behind forever.

Tom Ed was still back in Texas in his story. "I swear, sometimes I think Daddy forgot what my name was. Anyway, then JJ went to Nam. He came back missing a leg. He lost it rescuing a guy from a swamp. Got shot on the way out. He came back a hero. At least the government said he was a hero but he wasn't the same person. He was like one of those dogs you see tied up with an old piece of rope, drinking from a puddle, all nervous and then you feel sorry for them and you go to pet them and they snarl and bite you.

"Of course I was going to go. In his place. I was going to get revenge on those gorillas, I was going to be a hero, too.

67

But then one night, he'd been home — oh, I don't know — six weeks? Woke up to the smell of cigarettes. I looked out my window and there was JJ, sitting at the picnic table in the backyard paring his nails with a penknife, ashtray full of butts. I went out there.

"First thing he said to me? 'Fifteen.'

"I asked what he was talking about and he said, 'Fifteen nails. Think how much time I'll save over the rest of my so-called life because I only have to cut fifteen nails. Twenty-five percent saving in personal grooming time.'

"Then he stabbed the table with the knife. Left it there, trembling. 'You fixing to go over there?'

"I said, 'Of course.'

"Then he grabbed my arm. Vice-grip hard. Crunching hard.

"Do *not* go. Don't register when you turn eighteen. Move around so the paperwork never catches up with you. Screw it. Go to your medical and tell them that you're a bed-wetter or a faggot. Do it or I'm going to hurt you so bad that they won't want you.'

"Thing was, I knew that he meant it.

"The other thing was — that night? For that few minutes he was there. Next day he was gone again."

"Gone?"

"Yeah. He'd be sitting there but there was nobody inside his body. Nobody behind his eyes. Whatever that is? The self? The soul?"

Tom Ed looked up and gave Charlotte a sad smile. "The part of you that is you even if you have different teeth? JJ lost that in some jungle. A few weeks later he gave me a roll of money and said, 'Go to Canada.'"

"What's he doing now?"

"Don't know. He was supposed to go to college. He called it the cripple scholarship. But he flunked out. His girlfriend from before? She left him."

"Because of the leg?"

"No, 'cause he was acting like a total asshole. Oh, sorry."

"It's okay. I'm not Miss Biscuit."

Tom Ed gave his head a shake. "I don't know why I'm telling you all this."

They sat in silence for a while. But the world was never really silent.

"Hey, Tom Ed. What can you hear right now?"

"Leaves. You?"

"Traffic. You?"

"Some radio somewhere. Listen. Raindrops keep falling on my head. Dumbest song ever. Your turn."

"There's some kind of hum."

"I'm getting clouds scraping against the sky."

"The grass growing."

"The tree growing."

"My bones growing."

seven

Tuesday morning Charlotte woke to the sound of rain blowing against the window. She turned over and went back to sleep. When she finally wandered down to the kitchen, Uncle Claude already had a batch of chicken pies in the oven and was sitting at the table with a cup of tea. He pushed aside the scattered newspaper to make room for her cereal bowl.

Charlotte dug around for her favorite part of the paper, Ann Landers. Ann advised a mother who had been lending her grown-up son too much money that she should wake up and smell the coffee.

Charlotte topped up her milk. Family problems and Rice Krispies made a good combination.

She was just moving on to the funnies when Tom Ed came through the kitchen door.

"Got me a job. Car jockey."

"Frost my socks," said Uncle Claude. "That was quick work. No grass growing under your feet. You Americans are like that. In the bush, too. Go-getters."

Car jockey? Charlotte was trying to make sense of small men in bright silk outfits straddling race cars.

"Like in races?"

"No. I just move cars from lot to lot. It's a big car dealership. It's a three-to-nine shift. And I could pick up something else for mornings."

"Well done," said Claude.

"I don't start till tomorrow," said Tom Ed. "So today I'm going to work on becoming a Canadian."

Uncle Claude poured a mug of tea and handed it to Tom Ed. "What's your approach to that?"

Tom Ed pulled out his dodger booklet.

"Look, it says right here: 'Six books to describe a country.' Professor W.D. Godfrey, University of Toronto. Is there a library around here?"

"That's Charlotte's department," said Uncle Claude. "She's the reader."

Charlotte picked up the booklet. "Looks like Main Library stuff to me. Do you have time?"

"Sure. Can you point me in the right direction?"

"Well, you'll need a library card and for that you need proof of address. You could use my card but they might wonder if your name is really Charlotte."

"There's always a boy named Sue," said Uncle Claude.

"Johnny Cash!" said Tom Ed.

"Hang on, I can just take you and then I'll borrow the books on my card."

"Well, thank you!"

Charlotte left them singing some crazy song about a mean dad and went to get dressed.

{l}

"I feel funny carrying an umbrella. Like I'm being some show-off English lord or something." Tom Ed did look awkward as he dodged the other umbrellas on the sidewalk on their way to the bus stop.

"Sorry about the sunflowers. There was a black umbrella there the other day but it's disappeared. I think they just run away from home in the night. Don't you have umbrellas in Texas?"

"There's not really a need."

"Well, some boys think it's not cool. They'd rather get wet. It's one of those dumb boy rules. Oh, good, here's the bus. Shake out your umbrella before you get on or you'll drip on people's feet."

Charlotte smiled as Tom Ed tried to get the umbrella down while still holding it over his head. Who knew that using an umbrella was a learned skill?

The back seat on the bus was empty.

"Best seat," said Charlotte. "You can see everything that's going on."

"Like?"

"Well, like faces. Have you ever thought how weird it is that everybody's face has the same basic bits — two eyes, one nose and a mouth — but there's millions of combinations and mostly, except for identical twins, and even then if you've ever known identical twins like I knew Ricky and Mark Russo in grade three you can tell them apart?"

"Yeah, I have thought about that. The faces thing. Mom says I look like Daddy but I can't see it."

"You probably don't *want* to look like him."

Tom Ed looked startled and Charlotte gulped. She hadn't planned on saying something so personal. Was that rude? Maybe Tom Ed didn't want to be reminded of their conversation yesterday about his father and the belt and all that.

"Sorry. That was kind of ... you know ... not my business."

"No, it's okay. You're likely right." Tom Ed turned to stare out the window for a second, then seemed to wake up. "How old are you, anyway?"

"Thirteen."

"Hmmmm. You don't exactly seem like a teenager."

"You mean young?"

"No. Not young. Not old either. Just ... not a teenager."

"But that's perfect! Dawn and me? We've got this deal. We're not going to be teenagers just because we turned thirteen. We're going to skip it. We're going to be Unteens."

"How do you figure on skipping it?"

"Okay. Here's the plan. It's like hopscotch. Do you have hopscotch in Texas?"

"Sure do."

"Okay, so let's say the teenage stage is like square number five in hopscotch. One is being a baby. Diapers, floppy neck, baby powder, formula."

Tom Ed nodded. "And spitting up. Randy was a very barfy baby."

"Hop on one foot and you're on the second square, which is preschool — walking and talking, puzzles, macaroni, the swing set, eensy-weensy spider. You balance there for a bit then jump and land on two feet on three/four. That's being a kid. Reading, back roll into pike, pizza, bikes, horses, well ... horses in my dreams."

"Collecting rats for Duane."

"Yeah. All good, right? *Then*. Dum-di-dum-dum. Suddenly, there's square number five. *Teenager*. According to movies, books and my own observation, square five is bad moods, zits, pretending to be dumber than you are (or maybe actually becoming dumber), and being stupid and fake on the subject of boys."

Tom Ed snorted. "And football and getting beat up."

"Then one jump and you're back on two feet with six/seven. Grown-up life with money, your own car, your own apartment, ungreasy hair, freedom, university. I can't *wait* till university. I'm going to take *nothing* that you can take in school. I looked through James's calendar. I'm going to take philosophy, geophysics, sociology, theater and Russian. Then in the summer I'm going to backpack to see the Taj Mahal, and I'm just going to get ahead with the story and not be sucked down and teenagerized by, like, did Nancy tell Linda to tell Judy that Colleen likes Wayne."

"I can see you've given this considerable thought. But ..." Tom Ed hopscotched his fingers on his knee. "What about eight? There's an eighth square, isn't there? A single at the top?"

"Yeah, that's canes and see-through hair but you can stay on six-seven for *decades*. So here's the deal. Skip five and make a double-footed jump right into six/seven."

Tom Ed nodded. "I know just what you're talking about. Three/four you need a lifeguard. Six/seven you can *be* a lifeguard. What's the point of five?"

Charlotte pictured the previous summer on the beach at English Bay. What had always been long days of swimming, paddleboards, seaweed wigs, burying your friends in sand and sharing an order of chips had turned into tans and who's got a two-piece and whose towel was next to whose towel.

"Yeah, on five all you can do is flirt with the lifeguard."

Tom Ed grinned. "My daddy says they are the best years of your life. I don't know if they were for him or if he just has amnesia. But he doesn't have any idea. You go ahead, Miz Charlotte. Jump to whatever square you want."

{l}

Charlotte and Tom Ed tackled the big card catalog and found the call numbers for all the books to turn Tom Ed into a Canadian. Then they divided up the search.

"See you back here in half an hour," said Charlotte.

Charlotte had good luck. The books practically jumped off the shelves into her hand. It looked as if not that many people were taking out books in the Canadian identity section. With time left over she made a quick visit to the Teen Scene section. Revolting name but there were some good books there.

Tom Ed appeared back at the catalog with an armload of books, records and magazines. They found a table.

"Records! This is great. We don't have this kind of library at home."

Charlotte flipped through the records. On one cover there were four bearded guys in dresses. The Mothers of Invention. One was called Frank Zappa. They looked goofy.

"You like this band?"

"I've never heard them. They didn't play them on the radio back home."

"James would probably like it."

"James? Why's that?"

"See the title? 'We're Only in It for the Money.' Since he went into Commerce he believes that only money makes the world go round, that money is behind everything."

"He maybe has a point there."

"Yeah, but it makes him so grumpy."

Tom Ed ticked off his list. "Looks like I've got all the books to turn me into a Canadian. And I found one for you. I think it's about Unteen."

He pulled a book out of the pile. *Coming of Age in Samoa.*

Charlotte read the back cover. There was a photo of a woman, an anthropologist. Margaret Mead. She looked smart and kind and like she didn't care about diets or crocheted beach cover-ups. She had gone to live with people in Samoa and study their ways.

"Where's Samoa?"

"I'm not rightly sure. South Pacific somewhere."

Charlotte flipped to the introduction and glanced down the page.

"Why did you think ... Hey! They don't have teenagers there! Girls just go from being kids to being adults. Listen to this. The 'disturbances that vex our adolescents' don't happen there. Where did you find this?"

"I saw it on a display and then I remembered reading about Margaret Mead in *Ladies' Home Journal*."

"You read *Ladies' Home Journal*?"

"Well, it was, you know, sitting around. Mother got it. There's some interesting stuff in *Ladies' Home Journal*. Long as Daddy didn't catch me reading it."

"They should have this in the teen section. They should have a dozen copies."

Tom Ed nodded. "Thought you'd like it."

Charlotte took another look at Margaret Mead. Was it possible that there was a whole society of girls on the other side of the world who didn't have to do adolescence because they had never heard of it?

eight

The next morning the glorious run of sleeping in was over. Dad shook Charlotte awake at eight.

"Sorry, kiddo. Crisis at the store. I've got to pick up a load of mixed tropicals and Mom's got one of her heads. Can you come and help out, just for an hour or so?"

"What about Miss Biscuit?"

"It's Wednesday."

Wednesday Miss Biscuit went to a prison to teach criminals to read.

"What about James?"

"He's got something on at school. Believe me, Charlotte, I've already considered all the other possibilities."

Dad sounded fed up. He often did sound fed up when Mom had a migraine. Charlotte knew it was because he couldn't stand seeing her in pain, but it came off as grumpy to everybody else.

She allowed herself a sigh. Okay, it *was* kind of a teenage sigh but, honestly, since James had turned into Mr. Commerce-know-it-all he was *always* somewhere else when something needed to be done.

She stuck one leg out from under the covers. "All right."

Tom Ed was in the kitchen drinking orange juice and poring over his booklet.

"Okay, here are the occupations in strong national demand: Surgeon. Steel plate bender. Cutter, ready-to-wear garments except leather. What have they got against leather? And how come you're up so early?"

Charlotte explained about mixed tropicals, headaches, prison visits and her conveniently absent brother.

"Can I come? My shift doesn't start till three. I'd like to see the house-plant business from the inside."

The morning took a turn for the better.

{l}

"Show Tom Ed the ropes, okay?" Dad said. "And if you get a minute, you can mark down the lilies. I'll be back in an hour or so."

Charlotte handed Tom Ed a spray bottle. "Just don't spritz the African violets."

Half an hour until opening. Lights on, blinds up, coffee plugged in. The morning routine was automatic. When Charlotte circled back to the cash desk, Tom Ed was still standing there, holding the spray bottle.

"Uh, African violets? We haven't had the pleasure of being introduced."

Charlotte giggled. "Never mind. It wouldn't really matter if you murdered the African violets because nobody buys them anyway."

"Then why do you stock them?"

"They are Miss Biscuit's favorite. They're actually more like family members than merchandise. Just like the macramé plant hangers. We only sell one in a blue moon but Miss Biscuit likes to make them. Drives James crazy. He wants the store to be way more efficient and run according to business principles and he thinks we should hire people with more dynamic sales skills. But Dad and Mom would never fire Miss Biscuit because without this job their pension wouldn't stretch."

"Okay, can you teach me everything I need to know in ..." Tom Ed looked at his watch, "twenty minutes?"

"Sure. But what you need to know isn't about plants but about customers. Basically you get four kinds of people. You get your hippies. You get people who treat their plants like pets and play music to them. You get health-food types who use plants for medicine. And you get people who are buying plants for their downtown offices or swanky apartments. Really we only make money from that group because they buy the big stuff."

There were customers at the door right at opening, a couple from group four. The woman gave a quick, mouth-only smile when Charlotte unlocked the door and said good morning.

"Anything I can help you with?"

"We'll ask," said the man firmly, flicking raindrops off his coat.

Right. Charlotte joined Tom Ed behind the desk and began to flip through a plant catalog. Behind the desk was an excellent vantage point for snooping and eavesdropping. It never occurred to customers, especially the ones who didn't see you, that you could see them.

"I don't know," said the woman. "Plants seem so ..." she wiggled her fingers in the air, "fussy."

The man nodded. "No little pots. Can't stand all these little pots. We want to make a bold statement, but minimalist."

"Weeping fig," Charlotte said in a low voice to Tom Ed. "Just watch. They'll buy a weeping fig. They're weeping fig kind of people."

"So don't you want to go nudge them a bit?"

"Nah. They said they'd ask if they needed help."

"Maybe they don't know they need help. Which ones are the weeping figs? Let me give this a try."

Seconds later, Tom Ed was ma'am-ing and y'all-ing away for all he was worth in the weeping fig corner. The swanky couple started to blossom like giant hibiscus.

Charlotte watched in admiration. Tom Ed told them exactly what they had told each other about fussy and bold statements but he told them in Texan and they nodded like crazy.

"Three's what you need. *Wun* dudn't say anythang. Three says *stahl*."

After some more Texan sales talk the couple decided on three non-variegated weeping figs and three expensive black pots.

"Lots of light. Don't move them around. Don't overwater," said Charlotte as she dealt with their credit card.

The Swanks left happy.

"Wow," said Charlotte. "Big sale and it's only 10:30."

Tom Ed grinned and shrugged. "I think I deserve some coffee. You?"

Charlotte shook her head. She and Dawn had tried to like coffee but they agreed that even with lots of cream and sugar it still tasted like mud.

"You have it. I'll get a Coke. There's usually some hidden in the cooler behind the roses."

Tom Ed had wedged himself on a stool between the desk and the wall.

"So, Mr. Salesman of the Month, how did you do that?"

"You just pretend. You park your real self and put on a salesman self. It's like make-believe."

"But isn't that kind of phony?"

"Phony? I guess, but it's not like that self isn't there some-where. You just tune in the station and turn up the volume."

Charlotte slurped her Coke. "Parents always say be your-self, like that's easy. Which self?"

"Not *my* parents. Well, not my daddy, anyway. He'd never say be yourself. His whole thing is Be Me."

After such a promising start, business slowed to a halt. Cars swished by on the wet street. Umbrellas blossomed.

Tom Ed wound his legs around the stool. "I'd say you're pretty good at being yourself."

"Me?"

"Yeah. That whole Unteen thing. You're not just playing along with what everybody expects. That takes gumption."

Charlotte grinned. "Gumption! Nobody says gumption."

"I do. Gumption, gumption, gumption, gumption, gumption ..."

Coke went up Charlotte's nose. "Stop!"

"Gumption, gumption, double gumption, gumption ..."

There was a clatter from the back door and a gust of cool air.

"Dad's back."

Tom Ed unwound himself from the stool.

"I'll go give him a hand. Thanks for the talk, Miz Charlotte."

Time to mark down the lilies. Charlotte scrambled around in the desk drawer for the label thingy. Purple tape would be appropriate.

EASTER LILIES, *ker-chunk, ker-chunk*. 50% OFF. She felt daydreamy and totally awake at the same time.

The thing about talking to Tom Ed was that it wasn't like talking to a boy. Not that it was like talking to a girl. Also, it wasn't like talking to a grown-up but it wasn't like talking to someone her own age either.

It was just talking. Talking to a human person. A human be-in.

{I}

Time out of time. Thursday and Friday morning Charlotte hung out with the Texan human be-in. She took to getting up earlier. He made iced tea, which he just called tea because normal tea was called hot tea.

Tom Ed had questions about Charlotte's parents.

"Why do they sometimes say *thee* instead of *you*?"

"It's a Quaker thing. It's called plain speaking. My grandmother, the one who died, always spoke that way. But Mom and Dad don't really do it anymore except when it sometimes slips out. I don't even notice."

They listened to the Mothers of Invention, the strangest music Charlotte had ever heard, full of screeching and creepy whispering. (James, wandering by, said "pretentious garbage.") They talked about everything under the sun — the nuclear bomb, really good cars, letters in Ann Landers, Martin Luther King, what cats thought and were we just a bunch of atoms whirling around.

Afternoons and evenings Charlotte did all the holiday stuff. Badminton, a really stupid movie called *The Computer Wore Tennis Shoes*, shopping, daytime TV and babysitting. She was slogging her way through adolescence in Samoa but it was turning out to be a big disappointment.

Friday morning she did a preview report for Tom Ed while they sat on the back porch.

"It's no good."

"How come?"

"Sure, the girls don't have to do the teenager thing but they have to work all the time. Lola and Mala and Siva, they don't have much of a life. They have to grind coconut and weave and carry water and go on errands but mostly they have to babysit."

"You babysit. You babysat last night."

"Yeah, but it's only for a few hours and I get paid. Plus snacks and good TV. Those girls have to keep the little kids out of trouble and keep them from crying and bugging the adults all day long. They get to have a bit of fun around age seventeen and then they get married and have babies of their own and then it's work, work, work again. Boys have it much better in Samoa."

"Wake up and smell the coffee, Charlotte. Men have it better everywhere. More power, more money."

"Maybe, but I wouldn't want to be a boy because they have all these stupid rules."

"Rules?"

"Yeah. It's like the commandments of being a boy. Thou shalt not carry a lunch kit. Thou shalt not have a kickstand on your bike. Thou shalt not carry an umbrella. Thou shalt not wear a shirt and pants that match too much. Thou shalt not cry even if you break your collarbone falling off the monkey bars and it is actually sticking out or even if your puppy gets run over."

Tom Ed laughed. "Yeah, and thou shalt never lose even if it's something like how many times can you throw a peanut in the air and catch it in your mouth."

"It just seems so *hard*."

"It is."

"But girls don't get drafted."

Tom Ed pulled a pack of gum out of his pocket and held it out. Charlotte folded the stick in half and half again and started chewing.

"You've got a point there. But there's other ways of being wrecked by the war than being over there. Jimilene? She says the difference between men and woman is that women have to clean up the mess. Doctors do surgery. Nurses clean up. When babies poop or puke, daddies hand them to the mother to deal with. And those soldiers coming home from Nam, missing legs, crazy? Who's going to clean up that mess? Jimilene says women'll have to do it. She says women just have to go around with buckets picking up the pieces of what men break."

"Jimilene sounds smart."

Tom Ed nodded. "I miss her most of anyone."

"Charlotte!" The back door whammed open and James burst through. "Where the heck is my tennis ... Oh. What are you doing here?"

It was rude. What *was* it with James? Whenever he was in the same room with Tom Ed he got all prickly. Okay, so he didn't agree with draft dodging. That didn't mean he got to act like a jerk.

"Discussing women's lib with your sister."

Tom Ed sounded extra slow and drawly. Was he being rude back? Charlotte couldn't tell but what she could tell was that the conversation had become a code and that she was being left out.

Time to get things back on track.

"Did you have a question about your tennis racket?"

"Yeah, did you take it? It's not in the closet."

"Why would I ..." Oh. "Um. I think it's in the laundry room."

James just gave her the look — the hairy-eyeball look.

"There was this dead bird in the raspberries and I used the racket to get it out and then I took it into the laundry room to wash the dead bird germs off it and —"

"Right." James disappeared back into the house.

Tom Ed stretched and stood. "Okay. The cars are calling. See you later."

Charlotte checked her watch. Half an hour to *People in Conflict*. She shifted Puff to a different place on her stomach and stared at her toenails. Maybe when Dawn got back tomorrow they should do pedicures. There was so much to tell her.

She replayed the morning's conversation. Women's lib? Was that what she and Tom Ed had been discussing? How did he do that? How did he make her feel like she knew things about things she didn't know she knew about?

nine

Dawn was due home around ten the next morning.

Charlotte was hanging around the phone but Mom kept calling people on a list to volunteer for some Quaker event.

"Mo-om! I'm waiting for a call from Dawn."

"I won't be a minute. Nearly done. I'll just finish this phone tree and then I'll head on down to the shop."

Charlotte sat on the stairs and pulled pills off her cardigan. "I won't be a minute" was one of those sentences that was almost always a lie. It meant I *will* be a minute and probably way more when Mrs. Plumtree can't volunteer because she has sciatica. Another one was "Who cares?" which usually meant somebody cared a lot.

What were other guaranteed lies? Tom Ed would have some ideas. But he was at the car dealership, taking an extra shift.

"Claire, can you give me a hand here?" Uncle Claude's face appeared around the corner.

"Oh, okay." Mom crossed out a name on her list and retreated to the kitchen.

The phone had barely caught its breath when it rang again. Charlotte leaped for it. "Dawn?"

"No, Monique. Hey! Did you see it? In today's paper? It's Dorcas's mother. She's trying to get O.O. fired!"

"What?"

"I know O.O. told us not to talk about this but we have to!"

"She can't do that, can she?"

"I don't know. You should read it. I didn't really get it."

"Okay, call you later."

Mom reappeared brandishing her list. "Two more calls then I'm off."

"Where's the newspaper?"

Mom made a vague sweeping gesture. "Living room? I haven't seen it this morning."

Charlotte checked the living room and the cluttered dining-room table. She made her way through the jungle of the front hall and out onto the front porch. No luck.

In Dawn's house the newspaper was kept in the magazine rack. In Dawn's house they threw away the old newspapers. They didn't cut bits out of them and leave the rest on top of the fridge or stuffed down the chair cushions.

Using powers of deduction, she finally found it in the hydrangea bush next to the front door. The new paperboy didn't have a very good aim.

There she was on the front page. Mrs. Radger, hunched over a podium, looking both kinds of mad and pointing. Her eyes were scrunched up, her mouth didn't seem to have any lips and she had helmet hair a bit like Juliet's mother.

Charlotte sat on the front steps and scanned the article.

Mrs. Radger had a new campaign. Turned out that after hauling Dorcas out of class, she went around to libraries and found out which ones had a copy of *Catcher in the Rye*. Then, a few days later, she made a speech at city council and talked about the smut that children were being exposed to in schools and libraries and how some teachers were poisoning children's minds and that if Miss O.O. McGough would not purge her classroom library she would personally see to it that she was fired.

"Smut." Charlotte said it out loud to the hydrangea.

Good word. You could sound really angry and disgusted when you said it.

The faint sound of the phone brought her down to earth, and she went back inside.

Mom again! "Yes, that's lovely. A lemon loaf would be perfect. Yes, eleven o'clock. See you then. Bye."

Charlotte held the paper in front of her mother's face.

"Charlotte, what are you doing? Oh. Oh, my goodness. Poor Miss McGough. That's just outrageous. How did we end up with someone like Mrs. Radger on council? Oh, well, she just likes to make a noise. I expect it will all blow over."

Charlotte pictured Mrs. Radger flying across the sky, smiling liplessly, one arm outstretched, hairdo unmussed by the storm. Like Mary Poppins, except no umbrella.

"Mom! Don't you remember? I need to phone Dawn."

"Just one more call."

"But you'll start chatting and it will take forever!" Charlotte recognized that she was using the teenage whine but she was doing so deliberately, for a particular purpose.

"I'll stick to business. Honest."

Her own phone. The first thing that Charlotte was going to get when she landed on squares six/seven was her own phone.

Finally. Dawn answered on the first ring.

"Charlie! Your phone's been busy *forever*. It was the best, the entirely best week of my whole life so far and I have huge news."

Charlotte tucked the phone against her shoulder, put her feet up on the phone table and settled in. Dawn was obviously about to burst.

"It's about my hair."

"Tell."

"It's a long story."

Charlotte wound the phone cord around her toes. "Tell."

"So, on the second night of camp there was a costume party. Nobody really had costumes so we had to invent something, like a joke. Mr. Giesbrecht, the brass guy who's kind of scary? He just pulled his arms out of his jacket and kind of lurched around like a monster. And Mr. Nelson wore his conductor's suit and had a single cigarette in the pocket and kept going around saying, 'Bond. James Bond.' So I looked around to see what I could find. Marilyn — you remember Marilyn with the French horn?"

Charlotte didn't really remember Marilyn. In fact, she had never heard of Marilyn. But it wasn't a real question.

"Of course she had Vaseline to grease her valves. So I decided to go as a sea urchin. I gooped up the ends of my hair and it really worked. Even Helen, who was the flute player in our group and such a snob, even she said it was good. But then the next day I tried to shampoo it out. *Nothing* happened. The shampoo just slid off the goop. One of the nice kitchen ladies gave me vinegar and I tried that. It hardly helped at all. Then she gave me some dishwashing soap and all that did was make my scalp itch. I was getting desperate. Helen, who was over being nice, kept saying that I looked like a greaser and that I was an April Fool's joke."

April Fool's. Charlotte had overlooked it completely. No school and time out of time.

"That sounds horrible."

"Completely! Anyway, after a day of humiliation this string bass player named Serge came over. I hadn't noticed him before. Well, you never notice string bass players. They're all shy and hide behind their instruments."

"Hmmmm." Dawn was given to statements like this about musicians. Oboists were out of tune. Bass clarinetists were nerdy. Trumpeters were bossy. Charlotte couldn't argue because she failed recorder in grade three and didn't know any other musicians except Dawn.

"So Serge said he'd be happy to cut my hair. He said that his dad was a hairdresser and had taught him some stuff and that he'd been cutting his little sister's hair for years. So then I remembered that I was going to be a different person at camp and I decided to be brave so I said yes."

"You're kidding! You let some almost complete stranger cut your hair?"

"I know, crazy, but it worked. That afternoon, at break time, Serge set me up on the chair behind the auditorium and found some proper scissors somewhere and gave me a pixie cut! Oh, Charlie, you have to see it right now, right now this very minute and second. Can I come over?"

"Sure. I've got some news, too."

"Okay. See you."

{l}

"Do you like it? Do you really truly like it?"

Charlotte met Dawn at the front door and they went up to her room.

She really truly did like Dawn's new hair. It made her look light and floaty and ready for anything.

"It looks great. Kind of Twiggy. That guy's a good hairdresser. Hey, did you see the thing about Mrs. Radger?"

Dawn didn't seem to hear the question.

"But Serge? Of course, everybody found out about the haircut and he got a lot of teasing — hairdresser teasing. But then, surprise surprise, mean Helen stood up for him and started saying dumb things like how strong and masculine the string bass was. This is just the sort of sucky thing you would expect from a flutist. And then, no surprise either, Serge fell for it. Bass players are not that bright. Anyway, they spent the rest of camp wrapped around each other. I could have told Serge what a bad choice he was making because

Maxine in the second violins who is from Helen's school? She told me that Helen already has a boyfriend …"

Helen … Maxine … first chairs … girls who play trombone. What was that smell? Charlotte's stomach perked up. Was Uncle Claude baking? Muffins, maybe?

"Charlie? Charlotte!"

"Um, what?"

"Bangs down or bangs pushed back. What do you think?"

Charlotte thought it didn't make much difference but she knew the rules of the game. "Oh, pushed back. Definitely."

"I might have to use spray then. Otherwise they just fall forward."

Enough about hair. Charlotte was just about to bring out the newspaper article when Dawn leaned forward.

"So what about Dodger Boy? Is he still here? Which room does he have? Is he here now?"

"He's at work but he's usually here in the mornings."

"Did you get to hang out with him?"

"Yeah. We went to the library and did a shift at the store but mostly we just sat around and talked. He's easy to talk to."

"Luck-kee! Okay, so tell everything. Does he have a girlfriend back home?"

"I don't know."

"How can you not know? How can you spend hours talking to him and not ask? What *did* you talk about?"

"Everything. Music. War. Americans and Canadians. Women's liberation. Unteens. Whether people are good."

"What do you mean, whether people are good." Dawn sounded annoyed.

"Tom Ed says that he believes that people are born good and they get messed up by bad stuff that happens to them but that his father believes that people are born bad and they need to have the badness tamed out of them."

Dawn rolled her eyes. "*That's* what you talked about? Boring."

It wasn't boring. It made her brain stretch.

Dawn tucked her hair behind her ears. "Anyway, that's not the kind of thing you talk to boys about!"

"He's not a boy."

"Of course he's a boy."

"I mean he's not a boy like that. He's not like a how-to-talk-to-boys boy."

"How to Talk to Boys" was the name of an article from *Seventeen* that had gone around the grade-seven girls. Charlotte had made fun of it and Dawn had joined right in. What was happening to her friend?

Dawn pushed back her bangs. "Well, it sounds pretty boring. Of course he's really polite."

"He wasn't being *polite*. And anyway, not as boring as Helen and Marian and a whole bunch of other people that I've never even heard of and that have made you start talking like a *teenager*."

"Marilyn! Not Marian, Marilyn. Sorry that I *bored* you. Besides, Charlotte, when are you going to get over the Un-teen thing?"

95

Get over it? Unteen was their best thing. Their best idea. It wasn't something to get over. How long had Dawn been thinking this way?

"You're mad."

"I'm not mad. I'm just saying that it's time."

The thing about Dawn was that she would never give an inch in an argument, never not once. She would never even admit that an argument was going on. Charlotte knew she was just the opposite. She could smell the faintest whiff of tension at fifty paces and she just couldn't stand it so she would do any kind of patch-up dance to make it go away. It was the way she and Dawn were together.

But giving up on Unteen?

And anyway, why was she always the one doing the patching?

She looked over at Dawn, who was rearranging the shells on the windowsill.

It wasn't just the new hair. She looked like a total stranger.

Ten

The kitchen counters were crowded with baking. The sink was full of bowls and a floury Uncle Claude was punching down some dough.

Dawn had left. Charlotte had tried a patch-up, changing the subject back to hair, but it was all stilted and stupid.

Charlotte stood in the kitchen door and felt like crying. Punching something also looked good.

"Can I help?"

"Sure. Good timing. Knead this."

The dough rolled under Charlotte's hands, smooth and soft and springy.

"How come you're making so many things at the same time?"

"I'm going back to the bush tomorrow. Got the call yesterday. I'm baking for the freezer here. Survival food for you guys."

"You cook here and you cook up there. You should take a holiday."

"That's what Gloria says. She wants to take the Fun Bus to Reno. Maybe come summer."

Gloria lived across the line in Washington State. She had a mobile home and grown-up children. Sometimes Dad teased Claude about marrying her but Uncle Claude said that Gloria had had enough of husbands, which suited him just fine because he didn't think he was husband material. She and Uncle Claude went on holidays together.

"Dawn go home?"

"Yeah." Charlotte turned over the dough and slapped it down on the counter. The sugary smell from the oven was making her feel sick to her stomach.

"You two good?"

"Yeah. Well, no. She's mad at me but she's pretending she isn't."

"Hmmm. Too bad. You don't want to fall out with your friend. Why don't you invite her for dinner? The whole gang's coming, Miss Biscuit and all. Dodger Boy. Even James, if he can tear himself away from microeconomics. I'm thinking Swiss steak."

Charlotte hesitated. Why should she make the first move? Why should she do the patching? After all, Dawn started it.

But her stomach won. Anything was better than going around feeling like throwing up.

Dawn answered the phone excited and bouncy, happy to come for dinner. It was as though the morning had never happened. As though she hadn't gone all cold and too busy to hang around. As though she hadn't left without saying "see you" or "phone me."

When Charlotte hung up she spent some minutes untangling the phone cord. Her stomach had calmed down.

She was just going to forget the morning. If she could.

{l}

At dinner, Tom Ed was model polite as usual, complimenting Dawn's hair and asking about music camp and quizzing Miss Biscuit about their squirrels. As Charlotte watched him charming everybody and juggling his cutlery (for Swiss steak he used the side of his fork as a knife, a handy approach) she was amazed at how much she knew about him — small things that added up to big.

Were all Americans like this? So willing to tell you about themselves? Or was it just Tom Ed?

The feeling at the table was so good natured that even James got sociable.

"Did you drive any good cars today?"

As usual, he didn't look at Tom Ed and addressed his question to the bowl of scalloped potatoes.

"Sure did — '66 Dodge Charger."

"That was the last year with the Fratzog emblem on the grill as well as the trunk hatch, eh?"

"Nope, they had that in '67 as well. But, on the subject of cool cars, I've got a job tomorrow with the coolest."

"Sunday?" said Miss Biscuit.

"Yes, ma'am. They have to get a car to some place called 100 Mile House. Have you heard of that town?"

Miss Biscuit had indeed heard of 100 Mile House and they proceeded to tell a story about a British nobleman who built a lodge there, back in the old days.

"What's the car?" James asked the carrots.

"New Dodge Super Bee convertible."

"No!"

"It's a great assignment. I get time and a half for Sunday, expenses, and I get to drive one of the coolest cars in the world."

"Are you going there and back in the same day?" asked Dad. "That's a long drive."

"Yes," said Tom Ed. "I'll be leaving very early."

"Can I come?"

The words were out before Charlotte actually thought them up.

Everyone laughed. (Well, not James. He just looked annoyed.) But then it quickly seemed to come around to real.

"I'd certainly appreciate the company," said Tom Ed.

"Are you allowed to have a passenger?" said Mom.

"Yes, ma'am. They said I could."

It got noisy. Miss Biscuit was wondering if the luxury car was for the Marquess of something-or-other. Uncle Claude was clearing the plates. Dad was quizzing Tom Ed on his highway-driving experience. James was asking the pickle dish about front bumper design.

But there was one silent pool. Dawn, completely quiet and intense, was looking at Charlotte with laser eyes.

"Can Dawn come, too?"

Tom Ed did his slow smile. "That would be fine with me."

Of course then there had to be phone calls where Mom talked to Dawn's mom and Dad talked to Dawn's dad and then it made sense to have a sleepover because of an early departure and Dawn had to go home to get pajamas and a change of clothes.

{l}

"Where is 100 Mile House a hundred miles from, anyway?" Charlotte launched the question over the edge of the bed to floor level where Dawn was on an air mattress.

"Charlotte, we really need to go to sleep. We have to wake up at five."

Was Dawn being sensible or was she still being kind of mad?

"Okay. You're right. Goodnight."

Charlotte was the opposite of sleepy. "Maybe it's a hundred miles from Vancouver but I think it's more. Or you could go straight up a hundred miles and you'd be at, like, Sputnik. But they didn't have Sputnik when Lord Whatshisname went there so that can't be it."

Breathe, breathe, slight sniffle, turn over, squeak of air mattress. Sigh.

"Then again you could go straight down. Then you'd get to melted rock. Is there melted rock at a hundred miles? Is that magma? Or maybe it's called the mantle."

Exasperated sigh.

All right. Give up. She had offered silly and Dawn wasn't going to play along. Maybe she would unbend by tomorrow.

Puff settled into the crook of Charlotte's knees and purred. At least *she* appreciated Charlotte.

{|}

The Super Bee was amazing, bright yellow with a black band around the back and angry-wild-animal headlights.

"Top down?" asked Tom Ed. "It'll be a bit chilly first off."

"Down for sure," said Charlotte.

"Definitely," said Dawn.

The front seat was wide enough for three, even if the passengers wanted to sprawl around, which Charlotte and Dawn did.

"Who's this for again?" Charlotte asked.

"I don't know," said Tom Ed. "I'm just delivering it to a dealer. Maybe for that Lord somebody that Miss Biscuit was talking about."

Dawn raised both arms to the sky. "Oh, if only we would see somebody we know!"

"Who's going to be car-gazing at five o'clock in the morning?"

The Bee came into its own on the highway. It floated along all well behaved, but to Charlotte it felt like Puff when she was getting herself ready to jump up onto the kitchen counter, poised to do something bad.

The radio was playing quietly. Sometimes the rhythm of the song matched the telephone poles or the broken line on the road. Charlotte pulled up the hood of her jacket to keep her hair from flying all around. She tried to stay awake but her head kept flicking forward. Dawn had conked out against the door.

The Super Bee turned and slowed.

"Breakfast time," announced Tom Ed. "See that sign? Red's Diner. I think we can trust somebody named Red to do a good breakfast."

Red's was a busy place for so early in the morning. All the booths were full of guys in baseball caps so they took a table.

Tom Ed held out the chairs. Dawn lifted her eyebrows as if to say, "Wow, manners!"

"Just to be clear," said Tom Ed. "It's on me. I've got expenses."

Charlotte perused the menu. It was huge. You could have used it as a pup tent. She searched for the cheapest thing. It was nice of Tom Ed to treat but for sure the car dealership wasn't paying for three. The Quintanos didn't eat out very often and never for breakfast. When they traveled, which was almost never because of the store, they carried a kettle and ate from the big red cooler.

Toast. Toast would be good. There was a little caddy for jam on the table and it had both marmalade and peanut butter, Charlotte's favorite toast combo.

"Coffee?" said the waitress, coffee pot in hand. She was wearing an apron with frills. The frills didn't match her voice, which was flat and bored.

"Yes, ma'am. Thank you very much."

"Yes, please," said Dawn.

What? Dawn didn't drink coffee. So much for coffee tasting like mud.

"Um, tea for me, please."

"I'll go ahead, shall I?" said Tom Ed. "Lumberman's Special, side of pie and a Coke, please."

Coke! For breakfast! Not to mention pie.

"What kind of pie?" asked the waitress.

"You look like a person who knows her pie. What would you recommend?"

The waitress brightened. "Apple's good."

"Then apple it will be."

Dawn ordered the Sunshine Breakfast with the bacon option. After that it would have been ridiculous to just order toast so Charlotte followed suit. And if Tom Ed was having Coke, so were they.

Dawn sipped her coffee and dumped three more creams and a sugar into it. She shook out her pixie cut and leaned across the table.

"Is this what boys eat in Texas? Lumberman's Special?"

"Well, it's not called the Lumberman's Special because we don't have lumber. In fact where I come from we don't have hardly any trees at all."

"No?"

Charlotte jumped in. "Yeah, there's a town near where Tom Ed grew up called Levelland where it really is just level, with no mountains and no trees. If you stand on a can of tuna you can see to the edge of the state."

"Tuna?"

"More coffee?" The waitress was hovering.

"Yes, please, ma'am. This is fine coffee."

"What's that?" Dawn reached out and touched the back of Tom Ed's hand. A fine white line went across the back of the knuckles.

"That's from the shark-infested water."

"You got bitten by a shark!" Dawn's voice went up a few octaves and the ball caps turned.

"Imaginary shark. My brother JJ and I, we used to sneak into this yard next to the railway track and climb up on the cotton bales and run around, jumping from one to another. We pretended the ground was shark-infested water. Once I fell off and landed on a sharp piece of metal."

"We did that, too," said Dawn. "We made like a course around Charlotte's living room, jumping on all the furniture. We weren't allowed to touch the floor. We used the leaves from the dining-room table as bridges. Then one day I over-jumped from chesterfield to armchair and went right through the window."

"We didn't imagine sharks, though," said Charlotte.

Dawn frowned. "So I have a scar, too."

Dawn's scar was at the top of her leg. Was she going to offer to show it? And why was she hogging the conversation?

Tom Ed grinned. "Is a chesterfield a couch? I just love the words you use, all British-like."

With the arrival of the breakfasts, heaped on huge plates, talk turned to school. Tom Ed described how they learned all kinds of Texas stuff, like how to read cattle brands and about the different kinds of fences on a ranch.

"What's bob war?" said Dawn.

Charlotte laughed. Over the past week she had become good at translating Texan.

"He means barbed wire!"

"We also learned the positions in a cattle drive. You've got your trail boss, point man, swing, flank, drag rider and horse wrangler."

Dawn nodded. "Like we learned about jobs in the bush."

"Such as?" Tom Ed dipped toast into his sunny-side-up eggs.

"Um. High-rigger."

"What do they do?"

Dawn did a "help me" thing with her mouth at Charlotte.

"They climb up and cut off the top of the tree. It's the most dangerous job."

"And what else?"

Charlotte tried to remember. Faller? Was faller one of them?

"Saw chief," said Dawn. She winked at Charlotte. Dawn was an excellent winker. She could close one eye without moving any other part of her face. "He's in charge of sharpening the saws."

A giggle bubble rose up in Charlotte's throat. "Ringer. He counts the rings."

"Timber Voice, he yells 'Timber!'"

Tom Ed raised his eyebrows but Charlotte and Dawn were on a roll.

"Branch Manager, he manages the branches."

"Woody Woodpecker."

At that one, which made no sense at all but struck both girls as completely hilarious, Coke went up Dawn's nose and things got a bit loud and the baseball caps started to look over and the waitress brought Tom Ed's pie and more napkins and the bill all at the same time.

Over pie, Dawn told the story of writing the same essay, "How Is Plywood Made," for three grades in a row and Tom Ed admitted that he made do with reading the comic-book version of *Great Expectations* in high school.

"All right, you goofs," said Tom Ed. "I think we should get going. The Super Bee awaits."

Charlotte went to the bathroom. Everything was normal again. Dawn was back, saved by giggling. Two friends, one old, one new. Everybody eating bacon. What could be better?

She turned her wet hands under the roaring dryer.

There was one funny thing, though, about the last part of the breakfast conversation.

It wasn't really Dawn who turned in that plywood essay three times.

It was her.

eLeven

As they left Red's, Dawn stopped by a newspaper box to tie her shoelace.

"Charlotte! Look at this!"

Charlotte crouched down. There was Mrs. Radger. Smiling. Somehow smiling with no lips was even meaner-looking than frowning with no lips.

Councilwoman cleans up city libraries.

"Oh, yeah. It was in the paper yesterday, too. Monique told me. Mrs. Radger's gone completely nutty. Now she's trying to get O.O. fired."

"Why didn't you *tell* me?"

Tried to. Charlotte didn't say it.

Tom Ed slid some coins into the slot and pulled a paper off the pile. "You can read it to me in the car."

The wide seat was very handy. Charlotte and Dawn opened the paper out and reported in tandem.

Charlotte began. "*Miss Oona McGough …* Oona! I'd never

have guessed Oona. I thought for sure it must be Olive or Olga."

"We still don't know what the second O is."

"Prob'ly Opal," Tom Ed chimed in. "So, this is the O.O. who was probably a spy in the war, right?"

"What?" said Dawn. "How do you know about that?"

"Charlotte filled me in."

"That was *my* idea!"

Was it? Charlotte couldn't remember. Together they had added up O.O.'s comments about growing up in England and how she knew Morse code and how she had a limp because she had once jumped out of a plane in a parachute and how she lit up when one of the back-row boys brought in a book about code-breaking. Who had first thought of the idea of a spy?

It wasn't worth arguing about.

When they got back on the highway the wind threatened to snatch the paper out of their hands.

Dawn took over the reading. *"Miss Oona McGough, at present on paid personal leave, has refused to remove the novel Catcher in the Rye from her classroom. Disciplinary action has been taken."*

"What does that mean?"

"Maybe she got a detention."

"I think it means she's going to get fired," said Tom Ed from beyond the newspaper huddle.

Dawn turned to the next page. "There's more. *The teacher in question, with the support of her union, has threatened to take*

109

legal action. Wait! There's going to be a public meeting. At the school board offices."

Tom Ed pulled out to pass a camper. The Bee surged like a racehorse.

"You girls should go. Have your say."

Dawn lowered the paper and tossed it in a crumple on the floor. "No way José will they let students go to that."

"Why not?" said Tom Ed. "You're the public, aren't you?"

"Yeah," said Charlotte. "But they think we're just teenagers and adults hate teenagers."

Tom Ed grinned. "But you're not teenagers. You're Unteens, right?"

A silence blew through the car. Charlotte didn't want to look at Dawn. Dawn who had quit Unteens.

Had she?

Dawn leaned over and started to tidy up the sheets of newspaper on the floor.

Crinkle, crinkle. Fwap, crinkle.

Tom Ed shook his head. "Even if you went disguised as teens I think you're wrong about adults. They don't hate teenagers. They're afraid of them."

Dawn snorted. "Come on!"

"Adults think that teenagers are judging them. They think we think they're boring and stupid and irrelevant. Of course sometimes we *do* think that. But it makes them scared because deep in their hearts they think it might be true. At least, that's what I think that they think that we think."

It took a minute for Charlotte to get the thinks sorted out, but then it rang true. "If we went, what would we do?"

"Use your unique strengths," said Tom Ed. "Let's make a list. Miz Novak, please take a memo."

"Paper?" said Dawn.

Charlotte had taken a paper placemat from the restaurant because it had a funny map of British Columbia on it. She pulled it out of her bag.

"Okay," said Dawn. "Charlotte. You start."

"Unique strengths. Let's see. I can sing all the verses of the Mr. Clean jingle."

Charlotte sang Mr. Clean to the mountains and the clouds. "Floors, doors, walls, halls, white sidewall tires and old golf balls ..."

"What's the point of that?" said Dawn.

"Write it down," said Tom Ed. "You never know. List absolutely everything. Okay, Dawn, your turn."

"Um, violin. That's about it."

Was she sulking? "Come on, Dawn. You speak Croatian. That's huge. Write it down."

Once they started back-and-forthing, the unique strengths added up. By the time they ran out of room on the back of the placemat they had one pretty-good-at-badminton, experienced-at-tie-dye, jingle-singing reader and one ear-wiggling, winking, bilingual-English-and-Croatian, also-experienced-at-tie-dye violinist.

"You're missing some obvious strengths," said Tom Ed. "You have three powerful tools. You're young, you're smart and you're pretty. Write that down."

111

Pretty? Charlotte glanced at Dawn whose eyebrows were inching up toward her fallen-down bangs. They both started to giggle at the same moment. It was a complete, one hundred percent, classic teenage giggle. A proper Unteen would *never* have giggled that giggle. But it crashed over them like a wave.

Charlotte took immediate preventive action, grabbing the newspaper and putting it over their heads, holding it down as it flapped and snapped. In the privacy of their newsprint tent they rode the wave until it threw them up onto the beach of deep breaths and nose-blowing.

Tom Ed pretended not to notice. So polite.

"Let's get down to basics. Y'all like this teacher, right?"

The girls nodded.

"Then you could just go to the meeting and say that she's a good teacher and you want her back."

"I can't do public speaking like that," said Charlotte. "Standing up in front of all those people looking at you. I'd freeze. But Dawn can do it. I can give advice and clap."

"That would be good," said Tom Ed. "What with the qualities that I just mentioned and won't mention again it could be really effective. But I wonder if there's a way to make it more dramatic, more theatrical, to get more of a media splash."

"Theatrical? You mean with costumes and props like in a play?" Dawn was obviously thinking of dress-up.

"Kind of. I'm thinking of anti-war protests. Big numbers are good. Songs are good. But if you really want to get attention, something kind of jokey is even better."

"Like what?"

"Have you ever heard of a guy called Jerry Rubin?"

Charlotte remembered something from when James first started at UBC.

"Maybe. Something about a sit-in. James thought it was stupid."

"Ah, yes, James. Political protests aren't his thing."

How did Tom Ed know what was James's thing or nothing?

"Jerry Rubin is this anti-war protester guy who knows how to get in the news by doing absurd things. Once he dressed as Santa Claus when he was appearing before some hearing. Another time he and his friends ran a pig for president. We need something like that. Read out your list again."

The group plan grew as the Super Bee purred through the tunnels of the Fraser Canyon.

Yale, Saddle Rock, Sailor Bar, Alexandra, Hell's Gate, Ferrabee, China Bar. Two stops for bathrooms and chips and licorice.

It took all three minds but by the time they pulled into 100 Mile House, a hundred miles above the magma and below Sputnik, the plan was perfect.

Nobody was going to dress up as Santa. There would be no livestock. But what Charlotte was going to write for Dawn to say was going to save O.O. for sure.

They didn't spend much time in 100 Mile House. They had lunch and then they set off for home. The drive back was in an ordinary boring Dad-type car, hard-top. There wasn't room for three in the front seat and Charlotte was feeling sleepy after eating a big plate of spaghetti, so she chose the back and stayed there for the whole trip, leaning on the coats, falling in and out of sleep, lulled by the hum of the tires, snatches of conversation from the front seat, the sound of the radio and the prospect of a shared project with Dawn.

TWELVE

When school started again there were no worries about teasing Dorcas because she wasn't there. Rumor, in the voice of Sylvia who always had secret knowledge, was that Mrs. Radger had pulled her out of school and was going to do distance education for the rest of the year.

But O.O. wasn't there either. First morning back, sitting all casual-like on the edge of the desk, was this skinny cute guy.

A sub.

Larry came right out with it. "Hey! Where's O.O.?"

Nobody waited for the reply. More questions rained down.

"Did Dorcas's mom get her fired?"

"Did she quit?"

"When's she coming back?"

The sub looked kind of nervous. He had a little blink-blink thing going on.

"It's my understanding that Miss McGough has taken personal leave."

"For how long?"

"The length of leave is undetermined. And kindly raise your hands before asking a question. Please and thank you." He sat down in the teacher chair and straightened some papers.

In other words, he wasn't going to give them any real answers. Then he said, blink-blink, that it looked as though the class was rather far behind in the curriculum and needed to get right to work on the five-paragraph essay, which everyone would need to know for high school.

"What about my book?" Something had got into Larry.

"Your book?"

"Yeah. I read a whole book over Easter, every word, and it's my turn to talk about it."

There were groans from somewhere in the back. "Not world records again."

"Shut up, skuzz," said Larry. "It's a whole different book."

The Blinker cleared his throat. "Ah, yes. I've heard that you do a lot of extra-curricular reading in this class. So let's build on your competencies and work on turning a book report into a five-paragraph essay."

"No book reports."

"Pardon?"

"We don't do no stinkin' book reports."

Charlotte looked around. There was mumbling and nodding. Whatever had got into Larry had got into everyone, including her.

Who did this guy think he was, taking over O.O.'s class, making new rules? Even Sylvia had a stubborn look.

Without any planning, the class turned into a gang. It was a sit-in. They were *not* going to do book reports. And they wanted to hear what Larry had read over the holidays.

"Well," said the Blinker. "Perhaps as a transitional strategy, we could hear from Larry today."

Victory!

Charlotte tried to catch Dawn's eye but Dawn was staring out the window.

Larry read a few paragraphs about bull terriers. The Blinker didn't quite know what to say about *The Big Book of Dog Breeds*. But the class knew they could keep the discussion going if they used all of O.O.'s usual questions.

Neil jumped in. "Did you come across any new words, Larry?"

"Yeah. Pedigree."

"I'll look that up." Sylvia bounced over to O.O.'s giant dictionary with the tiny type and took out the magnifying glass. "Pedicular … pediculous … pedicure. Hey! Weeeeird. Pedigree is something to do with a bird's foot. How does that make sense?"

It was fifty percent sarcastic, fifty percent real and one hundred percent fun. The class managed to use up all the time until recess. At the bell, the Blinker looked like he didn't know if the students were building on their competencies or if he had just been faked out.

{I}

The next day, Sylvia, insider informant, announced that the school board meeting about O.O. was going to be that very week, on Saturday afternoon.

Charlotte grabbed Dawn at the recess bell. "Three days! We need to get moving."

"With what?"

"Dawn! Wakey, wakey. With the plan to save O.O."

"Oh, yeah. There's not that much to do, is there?"

"Are you kidding? I have to write the perfect thing and you have to read 350 pages to get ready."

"I have to read?"

Had Dawn not been paying any attention at all on the car ride?

"Okay. Maybe not the whole 350 pages, but enough so that you sound like you mean it. I've got the book in my desk. You could start over lunch hour."

"Yeah. All right."

Dawn sat with the book over lunch hour but Charlotte didn't see her turn many pages. Was it just too hard for her and she didn't want to admit it? Maybe Charlotte should just read bits out loud, but what with homework and Dawn's music lessons, where were they going to find time for that?

In the afternoon, while avoiding multiplying fractions, Charlotte figured out where the time would come from.

"Dawn. We need to cash in our skills points and we need to do it tomorrow."

Skills points was a thing that the principal had invented. All grade sevens took five hours off regular class to learn a practical skill. You got to choose. The engineer taught some boys about the boiler. Somebody's uncle knew about bee-keeping. Donna's mom came in and did a class on money and led a field trip to her bank.

"Book mending. James's girlfriend Alisha did it when she was in grade seven. I'll bet they still have it. You just fix beat-up textbooks. All day! I can read to you while you mend."

Dawn shrugged. She seemed to be in a very shruggy mood.

Mr. Zinck, the librarian, was delighted. "Book mending is an excellent practical skill and nobody has volunteered for it for a couple of years."

Wednesday morning, he took Charlotte and Dawn up to the attic of the school, to a mystery room piled with text-books that had exploded their insides. There was a pot of glue and some paintbrushes and a box of elastic bands.

Mr. Zinck demonstrated. "You just slip the paintbrush inside the spine of the book like this. Wipe up any mess. Then an elastic band to secure it until it dries."

It was certainly easier than banking and boilers and bees.

When Mr. Zinck left, Charlotte stood on a pile of *Streets and Roads* and pushed open a high window. Faint squeals floated up from the yard below. The primaries were having PE.

"All right. Secret weapon."

Charlotte pulled *Pride and Prejudice* out of her book bag and settled into an old wooden teacher chair.

"You glue. I read."

119

"So. This thing. Is Tom going to be there?"

It took Charlotte a second to think who Tom might be. Why was Dawn calling him Tom?

"Tom Ed? I don't think so. He'd like to but he might have a shift on Saturday."

"You asked him already?"

"Sort of. We were just talking."

"When?"

What was this? The Spanish Inquisition?

"This morning. At breakfast."

"You had breakfast with him?"

"Well, I was eating my cereal and he walked by. It wasn't like we were ordering up the Lumberman's Special."

"You didn't tell me."

"Tell you what?"

"Never mind. Just read."

Charlotte put her feet up on the radiator and started in on chapter one. It was like dropping in on a friendly neighbor. And it was a chance to bring Dawn along with her for the visit. They used to read the same books but not so much this year.

"Isn't Mary awful? Does she remind you a bit of Dorcas? She's so serious and *boring*! Dawn? Dawn?"

"Who's Mary again?"

"She's the third sister."

"Oh, yeah. Pathetic. I don't get it. Everybody's so mean and sarcastic in this book. Mr. Bennet's horrible to his wife. And he gets away with it."

"But Mrs. Bennet's ridiculous. She's so out of it. It's hilarious.

And she's not the worst. Wait until you meet the minister!"

"I just don't see what's so funny about it."

Charlotte shifted. The chair creaked. If somebody didn't find something funny you couldn't talk them into it. Plus, Dawn sounded mad. What was going on?

Dawn snapped another rubber band onto a copy of *Fun with Science*. "Why do you like this so much, all these mean, rude people?"

Now it sounded like an attack. When Dawn got in this mood it was no good fighting back. Charlotte swallowed a mad-back reply. Just answer the question.

"I just like it. Maybe because they are so the opposite of Quakers. It's kind of a relief."

"What've you got against Quakers?"

"Nothing. Quakers are fine in real life. But in stories … Okay, so Quakers have this thing about not judging. They work at it. Like, in Meeting. Well, you went there that one time. Did you notice that even when somebody says something really dull everyone just listens? You're supposed to avoid going 'yes, but, yes, but' in your head."

"I thought that was nice. Kind."

"Yes, but! Sometimes it's so fun to just admit that somebody is conceited or mean or stupid and to think of the perfect come-back. Like Mr. Bennet does. But it's just in a book so nobody gets hurt. It's the fun of pretending to be bad."

"Okay, go back to the mean people. But when are we going to get to the romance part? It's going to be Darcy, right? The one who's acting like a jerk?"

"It takes a while to get there. I'll skip forward."

Once Elizabeth and Darcy started falling in love Dawn seemed to relax, even joining Charlotte in hating the poisonous Miss Bingley.

By three o'clock Charlotte figured Dawn was enough in the Jane Austen groove that she could pull it off.

"This thing I'm supposed to read. Have you written it yet?"

"No. I'm going to work on it tonight. Maybe …" Charlotte was about to say that Tom Ed might help when he got home from work, but something made her swing onto a different path.

"Maybe we can rehearse it tomorrow after school. Why don't you come over?"

Dawn tossed her paintbrush into the glue pot. "Do you think Tom'll be there?"

Oh, good grief.

"Maybe." It was Charlotte's turn to be shruggy.

{l}

Normally Charlotte's school-morning routine was extremely efficient. She had figured out a way to stay in bed until eight o'clock and still get to school on time.

But Thursday morning Puff had other plans for her. At ten to seven she decided to launch herself off the dresser right onto Charlotte's stomach — a full four-point antelope-feet landing.

"Ooof."

Her job done, Puff made a fast retreat.

Charlotte squinted at the clock, turned over and tried to get back to dreamland, which had been something ingenious involving embroidering with Smarties. However, the trouble was that Puff hadn't exactly landed on her stomach. When Dawn got a see-through model of the human woman, one of the things that surprised them was where the human stomach was located. Nowhere near the bellybutton. *Way* higher. The part that people called the stomach was actually full of intestines of various sorts plus organs including the specific organ that was now fully awake, the bladder.

Sleep. Come back, Smarties! Charlotte distracted herself by thinking of the word organ and how weird it was that it was the same word as organ as in church organ. Or those Hammond organs. Like the opening music to that soap opera, *As the World Turns*. Yes, she had watched the odd show during her week of afternoon TV. In that show you heard the organ music and you knew something was about to happen.

The distraction stopped working.

On the way to the bathroom she noticed that the door to Tom Ed's room was open, his bed neatly made.

What was that dark spot on the toilet seat?

It moved. Oh, no.

Charlotte jumped back.

Was it? Yes, it was.

Charlotte knew all about the wonder of nature's architects and she had read *Charlotte's Web* because of course she would, namesake and all. But none of that helped. She just loathed spiders. It was something about the way they moved.

Skittering. They made her skin crawl. Arachnophobia. One of the back-row boys had presented a book on phobias in class.

Downstairs toilet it would have to be.

What with the bladder landing and the spider shock and making her way downstairs, Charlotte decided she might as well just stay up. She'd have time for morning extras like breakfast and blow-drying her hair.

Standing at the sink waiting for the water to run cold for a drink, she stared out the window letting her eyes wake up. The backyard was sunlit. The lawn was silver with dew except for a green track across it, curving around to behind the shed.

Who had walked across it?

Move over, Nancy Drew. Charlotte Quintan, girl sleuth, wandered outside to gather clues.

What she saw when she rounded the corner of the shed didn't immediately make sense. It was like one of those find-the-hidden-picture games. You had to look twice to see the upside-down raccoon hidden in the leaves of a tree.

James and Tom Ed were there, Tom Ed with his back to her, James facing. They were wrestling.

No. Not wrestling. Hammerlock, half nelson? No.

They were kissing.

Charlotte was trapped, frozen between needing to stare, to make it make sense, and wanting to disappear.

Her brain had just sent the message to her feet to swivel and go when James shifted and looked over Tom Ed's shoulder. His eyes met hers, an electric shock of a glance.

Charlotte didn't decide to run away. It just happened and she was back in her room, her pajama cuffs soggy around her ankles, a sing-song voice in her head.

James and Tom Ed sitting in a tree.
K.I.S.S.I.N.G.
First comes love …

Somewhere in the house there was this toy called a View-Master, a device with two lenses and a lever. When James outgrew it he handed it down to Charlotte, along with a box of discs. Grand Canyon. Wonders of the World. Big Cats. 3-D. You loaded the disc, clicked down the lever and you got the next picture.

Charlotte rolled up the legs of her pajamas, sat on the end of her bed and made up her own View-Master disc.

James at the dinner table never looking at Tom Ed. *Click.* Tom Ed saying "James" in that slow way. *Click.* The look on James's face when she asked to go along on the trip to 100 Mile House. *Click.* Tom Ed's brother telling him how to avoid the draft: "Tell them you're a bedwetter or a faggot." *Click.* A boy named Sue. *Click.* Frank Zappa in a dress. *Click.*

Then an image from the summer before. Cousin Patty was visiting. Twenty years old from Toronto. Walking along English Bay beach with James and Patty, eating chips and showing her the sights. There was always a row of muscle-men wrestling guys who sat against the wall working on their tans.

As they walked between the muscle and the water James started to tease Patty and Patty teased right back, "I don't think it's me that's getting the attention."

Charlotte had forgotten all about that confusing exchange. *Click.* Tom Ed and James at the corner of the shed. Hair. Hands.

Bright. Real. 3-D.

Thirteen

Doodling. At this point in the year you didn't really care what your notebooks looked like. You also didn't really care about people who played an important role in the foundation of Canada. Charlotte drew spirals as the Blinker tried to keep the back-row boys on task.

The questions just kept spiraling around. Was Tom Ed "like that"? Was James? What was that whole world about?

Charlotte didn't have much to go on. Of course she'd read about that man who went to Sweden and turned himself into a woman. There was Liberace and all that glitter. The subject came up at Meeting once and the Friends were all calm and accepting but Charlotte had heard the boys at school insulting each other.

However. James and Tom Ed? They didn't seem to fit any of that. They didn't seem girly or fancy. And when did James go from disliking Tom Ed to wanting to kiss him? What about Alisha, the girl James took to grad?

Charlotte hadn't crossed paths with James or Tom Ed before school, and what was she going to say to them when she did? Would James be mad at her? Had Tom Ed seen her running away? Did James tell him? Did anybody else know? If James could be …? She didn't even know what word to use if she didn't use the schoolyard insults. Homosexual? Five syllables made it sound like a medical condition. Astigmatism. Monique had that. Queer? Was that insulting?

If James, who she thought she knew better than anyone, could be queer, anybody could. Anybody single. She browsed her brain for single adults near and far. Miss Biscuit, one or both. O.O. McGough. Prime Minister Trudeau! Yikes. Was this one of those big secrets that everybody just somehow agreed to keep, like the fact that one quarter of all the women you see must be having their periods?

What else was out there hidden in plain sight? How many more upside-down raccoons?

A line of spirals ran off the edge of the page.

{l}

"Earrings? What do you think? A bit of sparkle? And maybe boots. Can I borrow your brown boots?"

Charlotte looked up from the rock she had been kicking all the way from school. "What? Sorry."

Dawn held out an open bag of chips. "I know I should look serious but still like a kid mostly."

"No, thanks, I'm not hungry."

"Huh? You're never not hungry. Oh, well, more for me."

Overnight, Dawn had obviously bounced back from whatever was bugging her. She was acting like a yo-yo these days.

"Do you think it's better if I read the script or try to memorize it, or maybe I should use those cards."

I saw Tom Ed kissing James. I saw James kissing Tom Ed. You'll never guess what I saw this morning.

Charlotte used to tell Dawn everything. Now she didn't know how.

When they came into the kitchen, Mom had her head in the oven. She was wearing her usual cleaning outfit of Claude hand-me-downs. She looked like a lumberjack.

"Oh, you two. Good. Time for a break. I've heard that there are ovens that clean themselves. How about the big-brains work on that instead of putting men on the moon." She peeled off her rubber gloves.

"Let's get out of these fumes, shall we. Hungry? Wait till you see the snacks."

In the living room there was a big flat box on the coffee table. Chocolates, candies, dried fruit, nuts, cookies, all in their own little compartments.

"Help yourself."

Dawn plucked a large chocolate cookie from the cookie zone. "What's with this?"

"They're a present from Tom Ed. News of the day. He's flown the coop."

"What?"

Dawn gasped. "Where to?"

Mom started patting pockets — overall pockets, shirt pockets.

"Here we go. He left a note."

She read it out loud.

Dear Mr. and Mrs. Quintan, James, Charlotte and Claude,
Thank you all kindly for your warm hospitality. You will
always be my first Canadian family. I have a chance to go
with some other Americans to Nelson. They've got a place up
there that sounds good. I had to decide in a hurry. I apolo-
gize if it is discourteous to leave without saying goodbye in
person. I will write when I get settled. My final check from
work will come to your house. Could you forward it to V.
Popoff, Box 242, Nelson?
Yours sincerely, Tom Ed.
P.S. Charlotte, I'm so sorry to miss the presentation on Sat-
urday. But I know that you and Dawn will sock it to them!

Dawn's cookie suddenly snapped in half, showering crumbs over her sweater.

Charlotte tried to make sense of the day. How could Tom Ed be kissing James at seven and be gone to Nelson by four? "Why would he just go like that?"

Mom helped herself to an apricot. "I'm surprised, I must say. It seems a bit abrupt. But I guess it's to be expected. He'll want to be with his friends. Lots of the draft dodgers are heading up to the Kootenays with plans to live in communes and such, live off the land. They can join the Quakers and the Doukhobors up there."

Dawn had picked up the note from the coffee table. Charlotte leaned over to reread it. Tom Ed had terrible handwriting. It looked painful.

Questions ran through her head like bumper cars. What did this have to do with this morning? Was Tom Ed running away? Maybe she had the whole thing wrong. Maybe what she had seen was a goodbye kiss. No. Guys didn't do that. And even in a split second and even obviously not knowing much about anything, she had seen that it wasn't a friendly kiss even if guys did do that.

"Cashews?" said Mom. "This is certainly the deluxe mix. I'd say help yourselves while you can because Dad and James will make short work of it."

James! What did he know about this? How was he going to feel having his name just buried in the family list? Or was there another note just for him?

Dawn stood up. "I need to go." Her voice was flat.

What? Why didn't Dawn want to stay and talk over the news? Why wasn't she brushing the crumbs off her sweater?

"What about the practice and the boots?"

"Oh. Okay, but …"

Up in Charlotte's room Dawn still didn't say anything. She started roaming around, touching things, rearranging stuff. Charlotte sat cross-legged on the bed.

"So?"

Dawn gave herself a shake. "How could he?"

"I know. He was always so polite but leaving without saying goodbye was kind of rude."

"Rude!" Dawn plunked down into the beanbag chair, which exhaled quietly. "Rude has nothing to do with it."

"What are you talking about?"

Dawn gave a big sigh. "Charlotte, do you really not know?"

Not know? About the kiss? How could Dawn know about that? And why was she sounding so mad?

"Know what?"

"Tom and I are, well, you know, we've got this ... thing. We realized on that trip to 100 Mile House."

"What do you mean? I was there."

"But you were asleep on the way home. We talked. Really talked. There was this other ... force. We both felt it."

Other force? Dawn was talking like *Love Story*. This was the kind of thing they used to make fun of.

What had gone on in the front seat of the dull Dad-car when Charlotte was dozing?

"Did Tom Ed ... like ... *do* anything?"

Dawn shook her head. "He didn't need to."

"What did you say to each other?"

"I told him that he seemed like a person with a secret."

This was nuts. Dawn wasn't the person who knew he had a secret. Charlotte was that person. And even *she* didn't know the secret on that drive.

"Why would you say that?"

"Well … okay, don't get mad. Remember I told you about that girl Helen at music camp? At the beginning when she was still being nice, before I became a greaser and not worth talking to, we had this late-night conversation and she told me this line. She said it was magic, a sure-fire way to get a boy to like you. So I tried it on Tom."

"A line! Since when do you use lines?"

"Since … stop being … you know, that way you get."

Charlotte took a deep breath. She wasn't really sure what was the way she got but she tried not to get that way anyway.

"But what did he say when you brought out the *line*?"

"He looked startled and then he really looked at me, x-ray eyes until he had to look back at the road. And then he took my hand and said how did I get to be so mature for my age and how special it was to have friends who really know who you are and accept you and love you. He said love."

"But, Dawn, he's nineteen!"

Dawn punched the beanbag chair and glared at Charlotte. "Oh. You're just like everybody else. Narrow-minded. How old was Juliet? Thirteen! Those are just numbers. I know I'll have to wait. Tom knows that. But we're going to wait together. Or … we *were* going to wait together."

Dawn's voice shrank and her glance wandered. She started to talk to herself. "Oh. Okay. I get it. He did this for me. He knew it would be hard for me with my parents and all that. So he's letting me have some space."

Charlotte bounced off the bed. *Just like everybody else.* How insulting. And stupid and dreamy was even worse than insulting.

She stood over the beanbag chair and tried to sound understanding.

"Dawn, listen. Tom Ed doesn't like you that way. Believe me. I mean he likes you. He likes us both. Like you'd like a kid sister."

Dawn, still gazing out the window, sighed. It was the sigh that did it.

"Maybe you've got a crush on him but it's not Romeo and Juliet."

Dawn's head whipped around. "Crush! I thought you of all people would be on my side."

"I am on your side but you're not the reason Tom Ed left."

It might all have gone another way if Dawn had just asked what *was* the reason that Tom Ed left. Charlotte had taken a breath to tell her.

But Dawn just rolled out of the beanbag chair and headed to the door.

"I'm out of here. Don't phone me."

"Don't worry. I won't."

The door slammed behind Dawn.

Charlotte yelled through the door. "And, by the way, his name is Tom *Ed.*"

Her throat was tight with tears. It wasn't a very good yell.

{1}

Dinner that night was strange. James didn't come home. Dad was working late. Uncle Claude was with the lumber-jacks, likely not cooking stir-fry. And of course Tom Ed was gone.

Charlotte couldn't remember a time when she and her mother had had dinner alone, just the two of them. They had cheese sandwiches and dill pickles.

It was tempting to tell her mother about the kiss and the fight with Dawn. It was tempting to just dump it all in her lap. But Charlotte couldn't even imagine how to start. It was all way too complicated.

"He left in a hurry but he took time to buy chocolates."

Mom nodded. "Yes, so well brought up. I'll miss that boy. I liked the way he talked. Whenever I go to turn on a switch I think, "Fixin to turn the lat own.""

"Yeah. Water on the wind."

"What's that?"

"The smell of rain in Texas."

Charlotte could feel Tom Ed already turning into a story, joining Lena and Frankie and Ludo and all the other guests who had come through their house. But she wasn't ready to tidy him away. He was more than a story.

Fourteen

Charlotte flipped like a fish. The pillow was too flat, the sheets were too tight on her feet, her hair was itchy, somewhere outside her window was a drip.

Where was James? Flip. Did Tom Ed really just run away? Flip.

And Dawn. What did Tom Ed really say to her on that drive? Was she still going to do the presentation for O.O.? Did "don't phone me" really mean don't phone me? Did she even want to phone her? Was Dawn firing her as a friend? Double flip.

It was a hamster wheel of questions as Charlotte watched the blue glowing numbers on her Indiglo clock slide gently from one moment to the next.

2:46. Puff started to make a strange sound. In the glo of the Indiglo Charlotte thought she saw something small at the end of the bed — something Puff was throwing around.

Her body was faster than her mind, or at least faster than the part of her mind that flashed the word.

Mouse.

She was out of the bed and out of the room before she was thinking. She might have been squealing.

There was a light under James's door. She knocked.

"Go away."

"There's something in my room."

James opened the door. He was dressed.

"What?"

"Puff got it. It's kind of dead but not quite."

"Wait here."

Charlotte waited by the door, peering into the half-dark as James went in.

"Puff! Give it here." James picked up Puff and tossed her out the door toward Charlotte, then kicked the door shut.

"Reeeowwwww." Puff returned to the door and started scratching, making a creepy *ack-ack* sound — a sound that was way too far into wild nature for Charlotte, who was afraid to even touch her.

There was scuffling and banging and then the door opened and James appeared with a Kleenex bundle in his hands.

"Okay now," he said, heading down the stairs. "I'll get rid of this."

Charlotte hovered at the door of her room, her toes curling on the cold floor. James clumped up the stairs again.

"Done. Go back to bed."

"What about if there's mouse bits or mouse blood in my bed?"

"Oh, good grief," said James. "Look. Take my room."

It was like Charlotte's feet were glued to the floor.

"Jamie? This morning, I mean yesterday morning. Behind the shed …"

His face snapped shut like a door. "Forget about it, Charlotte. It's not your business."

It was the hands on shoulders that did it. It was the steering push that he gave her toward his room.

James turned into everybody who was pushing her away or leaving her behind or disappearing. He was Tom Ed and Dawn and O.O. He was Serge the hairdresser and flute-Helen with her stupid "lines" and the whole army of teenagers marching in formation and all you could do was duck out of the way.

Her fist hit James's nose with a crunch, felt and heard.

The last time Charlotte tried to hit James she was about six. He just held her at arm's length and let her punch the air and roar with frustration. He laughed.

This time James gave a surprised "oof" and then leaned over and held his hand to his nose. Blood began to drip through his fingers.

"Jeez, Charlotte."

The anger drained out of her in one giant whoosh.

What had she done? Here he'd saved her from a not-dead mouse and she'd slugged him.

Girl Guide first-aid kicked in.

"Lean forward. Pinch your nose. Keep up the pressure for ten minutes. I'll get a towel."

James waved her away. "I'll deal. Just go to bed, Charlotte."

He didn't sound mad. He sounded tired, which was somehow worse. He went into the bathroom and shut the door firmly behind him.

Sorry. Sorry, sorry, sorry. Charlotte stood in the hall with her throbbing hand tucked into her armpit. Puff looped around her legs.

James wasn't coming out. She went into his room and slipped between the cold sheets.

{I}

Could things get worse? Charlotte tossed her pajamas into the laundry. Would this be the first day of her period? Of course it would. Her hand ached, her best friend hated her, she'd slugged her brother, her favorite teacher had been fired, the best house guest *ever* had disappeared and now *this*.

She stepped into the shower. Periods. She and Dawn thought the whole human reproduction thing was ridiculous. Why not just flip a switch or get a shot or something when you wanted a baby rather than getting ready for it every single stupid month?

At least, she and Dawn used to think this. Maybe now she thought this alone.

Why not just stay home? Mom would always write a note. You didn't have to be sick. She said, "You have the whole rest of your lives for the tyranny of schedules."

You just had to make sure you made up the work.

Except, no. Today was the hotdog fundraiser for the grade-seven grad trip to Rollerland. She told Monique she'd help.

Charlotte dried between her toes. All right. A plan for the day. Hotdogs and trying to mend things with Dawn.

Friend mend didn't happen, though, because Dawn wasn't at school. That was unusual because Mrs. Novak was the opposite of Charlotte's mom. In her rule book you were either in the Emergency department on life support or you were in school.

All morning Charlotte kept glancing at the empty desk. Was Dawn sick? Was she so sick that she'd miss the presentation? Or had she quit that already? Had she quit their friendship?

The day was a wash-out. In art her hand was too sore to hold the pastels. At the hotdog sale one of the mustard squeezers leaked onto her skirt. Three o'clock was a long time coming.

The phone rang just as she got in from school.

"Oh, Charlotte, I know this is short notice and I'm sure you've got something on, it being Friday and all, but we're in a pickle. Don's got this cocktail do. Did he tell me that wives were supposed to go? Not till today. I said to him, I said, 'Don, if we can't find a sitter why don't we just take the kids? Children's first cocktail party.' Ha! Of course I'd rather not go at all because, well, I've told you about his boss, right? *Such* a chauvinist. So I'll have to stand around and listen to bra-burning jokes. You know what that's like ..."

Charlotte didn't actually know but she appreciated being talked to like an adult.

"... We'll be home by seven."

"Sure."

"You are saving my life."

When Charlotte arrived, the Seeley twins were already in matching baby-doll pajamas, teeth brushed. They were adorable.

"Aren't they adorable?" said Mr. Seeley.

According to the Quintan Code this kind of praise for children should spoil them, but actually the twins were funny and sweet, brattiness score zero.

After three renditions of "Going on a Bear Hunt," each version crazier than the last, the twins put themselves to bed in their pink flouncy beds and Charlotte went to check out the snacks.

The Seeleys were the best babysitting people. They paid fifty cents an hour more than the standard and they left excellent snacks. This time the tray held a bottle of Coke, a Mars bar, a little bowl of almonds and a cupcake.

Charlotte poured the Coke into a martini glass and turned on the TV. Color and cable. *Bewitched? Carol Burnett Show?* It was the perfect way to tune out the mess that everything had turned into.

Mrs. Seeley drove her home ("Don's had a few") and gave a full report on the cocktail party. "They were sweet-talking a potential client. He was one of those men who says 'the wife.' You know the kind. The car, the house, the aquarium, the wife. But I was good. I didn't roll my eyes. Business is business. Oh, I just can't *wait* to get out of this girdle."

There was a police car in the driveway.

Charlotte's mind leaped. Accident or crime. There was never a good reason to have a police car in the driveway.

"What the ..." said Mrs. Seeley.

Charlotte was halfway to imagining herself an orphan when Dad appeared beside the car.

"Thanks, Joan. I was just about to phone."

"Anything I can do?"

"No, it's okay. Claire will call you later."

The policeman was a woman. She was sitting with a note-pad on her knee. Tom Ed's goodbye letter was on the coffee table in front of her.

Had something happened to Tom Ed? Had he been arrested for being a draft dodger?

"It looks like Dawn is missing," said Mom. "Officer Johnson hopes you can help."

Missing what? Oh. *Missing*. Like teenage runaway. Charlotte pushed some papers off the chesterfield and sat down.

"So, Charlotte."

On *To Tell the Truth* Charlotte would have guessed that Officer Johnson was a kindergarten teacher. She had a soft voice and red hair. But, was that a gun on her belt?

"When's the last time you saw your friend Dawn."

"Um. Yesterday after school. She came over. Left around five."

Mom jumped in. "Didn't you see her today?"

"No, she wasn't at school."

"The absentee reporting system apparently didn't function at the school today," said the officer. "The parents saw her in the morning but were not aware until after school that she was not in attendance. So, Charlotte. How did she seem yesterday? Normal? Upset about anything?"

Charlotte noticed that the officer had large feet. Oh, how could she possibly explain yesterday? She didn't even really understand it herself.

"Charlotte?" Mom moved to sit beside her.

"We had a fight."

"You did?" Mom moved even closer.

"What was the nature of this fight, Charlotte?"

Why did the officer keep saying her name?

"Honey," said Dad. "We're not looking to get Dawn in trouble. We just want to find her and make sure she's safe."

Safe? There were those scary runaway stories. Charlotte looked up from the police feet. "She ..."

She just couldn't quote Dawn. She couldn't say, "meant to be together." Even though it felt like a betrayal she had to use words that the adults would understand.

"She told me she has a crush on Tom Ed."

"Ah," said the officer, picking up the letter. "And that's this individual, the draft dodger who was staying here?"

"Evader," said Mom. "Draft evader."

"Now, Charlotte, is there a chance that Dawn has run away to follow him?"

Charlotte could feel three pairs of eyes boring into her. She shrugged.

"She might've. She didn't say anything to me but she might've."

143

The officer tapped her pen on her notepad. "Have you girls ever hitch-hiked?"

"No!" The policewoman had the whole wrong idea of who they were. Or was Charlotte the one with the wrong idea of who Dawn was?

"Right. That's it for now." She folded Tom Ed's letter into her notepad and stood up on her oversized feet. "And I'll take this if I may. Thanks for your help, especially you, Charlotte. In these cases the first twenty-four hours are key. Here's a direct number to call if you remember anything else or if Dawn gets in touch."

"How long has this thing between Dawn and Tom Ed been going on?"

Dad had gone off to phone the Novaks and Mom was pacing around the living room running her hands through her hair.

There was no Thing. Even if there was a thing Charlotte didn't know about it. She didn't seem to know about anything. Everybody was keeping secrets. Everything she thought she knew was wrong.

"Stop asking me questions!"

Charlotte was not a yeller. Mom stopped dead in her tracks and Charlotte's stomach took the yell as an invitation to get rid of the Coke and the cupcake and the Mars bar.

She just made it to the bathroom in time.

Then Mom was holding her head and giving her a warm facecloth.

144

"Oh, Charlie, I'm so sorry. No more interrogation. Promise. Come on, I'll get you some ginger ale."

The ginger ale trickled down Charlotte's burning throat. Curled up on the chesterfield under a blanket she should have been sleepy, but there were still buzzing bees in her head.

Dad got off the phone. Dawn had left a note for her parents saying she was okay and that they shouldn't worry.

"Which at least assured them that she hadn't been kidnapped," said Dad.

The police were trying to find out if Dawn was on a Greyhound bus but there were some fog issues in one of the mountain passes so they didn't know yet. Mr. Novak was ready to drive up there as soon as there was any news.

"Let's just hope that's where she is," said Mom. "Oh, Charlotte, if this was you … The Novaks must be beside themselves."

"There's not much else we can do this evening," said Dad, heading toward the stairs.

How was it possible to be so tired but not one bit sleepy? "I'm going to stay up for a while."

"Not too long," said Mom.

Charlotte turned down the lights and made a nest of the afghan and a couple of pillows.

Dawn wouldn't hitch-hike, would she? Nobody good was going to pick up a thirteen-year-old girl on the side of the highway and drive her to Nelson. Anybody good was going to phone the police and get her rescued. So that left bad people. Dawn would figure that out, wouldn't she? If she was figuring things out at all.

She must have taken the bus. Charlotte thought about the bus station — a big, grubby, glaring place that smelled like pee. How much did a bus ticket to Nelson cost? How long did it take to get there? Wouldn't she be there by now? If she wasn't on the bus where *was* she, out in the night, not at home?

She shouldn't have said crush. She said it to be mean, to put Dawn down. She was a bad friend.

There was no way to make a story when you didn't have enough information.

Charlotte stared into the hall.

Just *ring*, for pete's sake. Be somebody saying Dawn's okay.

Pride and Prejudice was sitting on the coffee table. Escape to Jane Austen.

It was all there, of course. Chapter forty-six. Lydia, the silliest Bennet sister, a total teenager, runs away with this army guy, Wickham, who turns out to be a jerk. She thinks he's going to marry her but he doesn't have any intention of doing so. Mr. Darcy goes off to rescue her and then he *pays* Mr. Wickham to marry Lydia, which Wickham has to do because he had sex with her. When Lydia comes back you would think she would be totally embarrassed but instead she's all "Neener, neener, neener, I got married before the rest of you. I win."

Charlotte tucked the book beside her. It was the neener, neener thing. The way Dawn had started acting so superior.

But what was she doing, thinking bad thoughts about Dawn when her friend was missing and might be in bad trouble?

Thinking in circles. Trapped. She needed to move.

Charlotte found her runners and made her way down to the basement. Maybe she could just jog around the furnace. But there, in a corner half-hidden by boxes, was an exercise bicycle. Every so often somebody in the family would decide to keep fit and use it three times and then give up.

She slid onto the dusty seat, reached for the handlebars and pushed down on the pedal. There was a crunching squeak but the wheel turned.

Notch by notch, she upped the tension until her heart was thumping in her ears and her thighs were burning. Push, push, push, push. Up some steep mountain road.

And then, just as she flicked the level from eight to nine, she heard it.

Briiiiing.

The sound was faint and it only rang once but it was still echoing in her ears when she reached the kitchen, stumbling on the final step.

"She's okay." Dad appeared. He had hedgehog hair and his dressing gown was inside out.

"She *was* on the bus and she's in Nelson, safe and sound. The Novaks are leaving to pick her up. Mum's still talking to Mrs. Novak."

Charlotte hadn't thought ahead to what would happen when the police found Dawn.

"Will they put her in jail?"

Dad smiled. "I wouldn't think so. They'll just keep her safe."

Safe. Every twitch and jitter drained out of Charlotte.

"What were you doing down in the basement?"

"Exercising."

Dad nodded and hugged her and gave her a scratchy kiss on the cheek. "Get thee to bed, Charlotte."

She only made it as far as the living room.

Fifteen

I'm here today to speak in support of ...

Charlotte stuck her spoon into her bowl and read over the presentation that she had written, the presentation that nobody would ever hear. She glanced at the kitchen clock. At two, when the meeting started, Dawn and her parents would probably be somewhere on the road home. Would Dawn be thinking of the meeting and how she wasn't there and how she had let Charlotte down? To say nothing of O.O.

She stuffed the index cards into her pocket and returned to the stove for a top-up.

James appeared behind her and peered into the pot. "Chili for breakfast?"

Charlotte examined his face. His nose looked normal.

"I was *starving* when I woke up and it was at the front of the fridge. Want some?"

James shuddered. "Chili before noon is just wrong. Hey, what was going on here last night? I came in around one and you were asleep on the chesterfield."

Charlotte filled him in on the Dawn drama.

James rolled his eyes. "Dawn's a dope."

Those three words made Charlotte feel weirdly cheerful but she automatically came to Dawn's defense.

"No, she's not."

"She's a dope and she pushes you around too much. Always has."

Since when had James even noticed how Dawn was?

James poured a cup of coffee. "Charlie, we need to talk about something."

The chili did a flip.

Charlotte gulped. "Okay."

"Bring your revolting breakfast out back."

They sat on the swings of the old swing set. James's long legs stuck way out.

"Now, make a fist."

"What?"

"Just make a fist."

Did James want a fight? "Okay."

James took her fist in his hand. "Wrong. Your thumb still hurts, right?

Charlotte nodded.

"That's because you tucked your thumb under your fingers." He returned the hand.

"Watch. Press your four fingers together and curl into your palm. Lay your thumb across the top out of harm's way. Try it. Okay. Good. Remember for next time."

"Where did you learn this?"

"Guy stuff."

"I'm sorry I hit you."

"Bad Quaker," said James, shaking his head. "And I'm sorry I said none of your business the other night."

He cleared his throat. "So, there's this place in the Student Union Building called SpeakEasy where they have student counsclors and you can go there and talk about stuff. Some days there's a sign on the door that says, *We're here. We're queer. Ask questions.* So, shoot. I'm here. I'm queer. Ask questions."

Charlotte gulped. Was she ready for this?

"Is it okay to say queer? That's not insulting?"

"It's okay. It's kind of ironic but it's not mean. Do you know about irony? Oh, of course you do. All that Jane Austen."

"How do you know you are?"

"Because I'm sexually attracted to men and not to women."

"But what about Alisha? Was that just fake?"

"Not fake, exactly. More like being dishonest with myself. That's the part that's not so simple. For years I tried to figure this out all on my own. I read everything I could get my hands on. I tried to solve it like a math problem. But there are some things that you can't figure out just by sitting in your room and thinking about it. You have to go and live it. That means you make mistakes and you get hurt and you can hurt other people without meaning to. You just have to go through it."

Can't go over it. Can't go under it. Can't go around it. Have to go *through* it. The words danced through Charlotte's brain. It was "Going on a Bear Hunt."

"Sounds scary."

"Yeah, but also amazing. You discover things about yourself. Besides, the other choice is pretending for my whole life, never being myself. Now, that's scary."

"Do Mom and Dad know?"

"Well, I haven't made an announcement. But you know how it always turns out that Mom knows everything? I'm pretty sure she suspects."

The answers just seemed to open more questions. Charlotte ran through the formula. Category one: zero percent. In fact, negative percent. Not only would they not get any status but they would get insulted, maybe even beat up. Ringy-dingy: Also zero percent. It's not like they were going to get married. What would they call each other? Husband and husband? Ha! Three: kissing: lots of percent obviously. Except if the whole point of kissing was to get busy making babies, how did that work with two boys? Then there was the big one. Souls and all that. That was still a total mystery.

In the meantime. "I thought you didn't even like Tom Ed."

"I didn't. Not at the beginning. I thought he was a slacker and a flake. I still don't agree with his politics. But, he's so damn sexy. Slow sexy."

It was the most grown-up thing James had ever said to Charlotte, the most equal-to-equal. She had to fight off the urge to run away or giggle. But no. Deep breath, bent knees, prepare for a two-footed jump from squares three/four to squares six/seven.

Slow sexy? She looked at the cherry tree and remembered Tom Ed swinging himself up into its branches.

"Yeah."

A black squirrel bounced along the top of the fence.

James flung the last few drops of coffee into the air. "So. What are you up to today?"

"I *was* going to that school board thing."

"Oh, I'd forgotten all about that. That business with nutbar Radger, right?"

"Yeah. And O.O. You know. You had her, right?"

James nodded. "What was the plan?"

Charlotte pulled the creased cards out of her pocket. "This."

James read for a few seconds and then snorted. "This is good! You had me! This is going to be fabulous."

"Except Dawn was going to do the talking part."

"Well, then, you have to do it."

"Come on. I can't even speak up in Meeting. There's no way I can get up in front of a bunch of strangers and public speak."

"Of course you can. You can read aloud, right? You can talk. You need to do this, Charlie."

"No."

It was as if she hadn't spoken. James was poking his finger at the notes. "It's actually way better for you to do it anyway, more effective. If Dawn the Dope said this it would be fake. But with you it's real. You've always got your nose in a book."

"They don't know that."

"But there's something about real. It shows. Mom and Dad going with you?"

"No. T —" Charlotte stumbled. Was Tom Ed a name she could just say in the normal way? "Tom Ed thought that if parents were there, then people would think they'd put me up to it."

"He's right. But I'll come if you want. As far as I'm concerned that guy in *Catcher in the Rye* is a complete whiner, but it's a matter of principle. We can't have Radger and her friends running the show. Besides, I liked O.O. What time's the thing?"

"Two, but —"

"Okay, we should get there early because there might be a limit on the number of speakers and we'll want to get you on the list. I'll call Dad at the shop and see if we can take the car."

How did it go from Charlotte saying absolutely no to an estimated departure time? Charlotte's stomach knotted into a round turn and two half hitches.

{I}

James was right. Twenty minutes early and the sign-up sheet was already filling up. First name on the list: Bernice Radger. Big bold handwriting.

There was still time to chicken out. Charlotte fingered the index cards in her pocket. Just being in the audience was still supporting O.O., right?

James handed her the pen. "Hurry up. We need to make sure we get you an aisle seat."

Charlotte Quintan. Number seven. There she was. Her own signature.

They found seats and Charlotte looked around. At the front, on a riser, was a table wearing one of those pleated table skirts. There were three chairs, microphones, glasses of water, binders, and two men and one woman, all in suits. In both aisles were microphones on stands. Off to the side was a man with a TV camera.

People were starting to stream in. Charlotte recognized a few kids from school but mostly it was adults. She couldn't see O.O. anywhere. In the front row one of the backs of the heads looked like Mrs. Radger. There was no sign of Dorcas.

It began when the woman read something from her binder about school-board policy and said how everyone was to be respectful and there was a five-minute time limit for each speaker.

Mrs. Radger hardly needed the microphone. Her voice was so loud that every time she said *P* or *B* the microphone made a little explosive pop. She read parts of *Catcher in the Rye*, some bad-word parts and some sexy parts. She seemed to be enjoying herself in the bad-word parts. Then she said her piece about moral filth. She used up all of her five minutes.

There was a smattering of applause, mostly from around the area where Mrs. Radger was sitting.

Just as the applause died down, Charlotte felt a tap on her shoulder. She turned around. Miss Biscuit!

The left Biscuit gave her a pat. The right Biscuit mouthed, "Good luck."

The second speaker was a weedy man in a gray suit who said all the same things as Mrs. Radger but with less drama and no sexy quotations.

From then on, everyone was on O.O.'s side. There was a woman reporter who had had O.O. as an English teacher in elementary school and said she had changed her life. There was a librarian who was also an ex-student. There was a professor of English from the university who talked about *Catcher in the Rye* and how it had an "exquisitely rendered character." James grinned at Charlotte. There was somebody from the teachers' union.

But Charlotte didn't really take in what they were saying. Every speaker, every word, brought her closer to her turn. She was on a train in a tunnel hurtling toward disaster, and there was no escape.

"Puintan, Charlotte Puintan?"

James nudged her. A Biscuit squeezed her shoulder.

In the eight-mile walk to the microphone, Charlotte thought about the capital Q. It was always a problem in handwriting, looking like a big 2. Maybe she should just have printed her name.

At the six-mile point her feet had disappeared and the top of her head was abuzz. The silence was booming. The people had disappeared. The room had disappeared.

She had to stretch up to the microphone.

"It's Quintan." To her own ears she sounded like a duck.

"Pardon me," said the school-board lady. "Charlotte Quintan."

A woman sitting next to the microphone reached over and twiggled it shorter. It gave a little screech.

Just say the first line. That's all you need. The first line.

Charlotte took a deep breath.

"I'm here today to speak in support of Mrs. Radger."

Something happened to her voice. It got fatter.

The school-board people looked up from their binders and blinked. But that wasn't all. Charlotte felt the room behind her click to attention. As the room came back, so did her feet and her head. Every little atom was alive, poking its head up.

She flipped to the second card. "I am here to make my own complaint about a book in our classroom library. I read this book because of the recommendation of Miss O.O. McGough, my teacher. When I read it I was disturbed to find out that it includes an underage girl having sex with a much older man. Furthermore, it encourages disrespect for parents. The mother in this story is portrayed as a fool and the characters are encouraged to make fun of her."

It was like she had eyes in the back of her head. She could magically see the people listening. She could smell it. Nose in the back of her head? One of the school-board men at the table met her eyes with a crackling look and started to smile. She pretended not to see him.

She flipped to the next card. "Worst of all, the church minister in the book is also portrayed as idiotic and boring. Through the whole book young people are disrespectful of parents and other figures of authority."

It was like walking the balance beam. She had to sound like a milder version of Mrs. Radger. She had to sound like she meant it.

"I think this book is bad for me and other teenagers because it encourages rudeness, insolence and other bad attitudes. The main character is an inappropriate role model. I therefore request that it be removed from our school."

It came to her in a flash, what do to next. She had the punchline but she needed to pretend to flub it.

"Thank you." She half-turned to go but wheeled back to the microphone just before the audience began to react. She pretended to be flustered. She was good at that because she had had lots of practice being flustered for real.

"Oh, sorry. I forgot to say what the book was. The book is called *Pride and Prejudice* by Jane Austen."

They started to applaud before she had even turned away. They applauded for the whole eight miles back to her seat and more. There was even some stamping and a couple of whoops.

She slipped in beside James. She was bigger on the inside than on the outside. She was the amazing expando girl.

{I}

"She was the hit of the whole event!"

They picked up Mom and Dad at the shop on the way home and James started in right away.

"She was so confident. Her voice changed. About two sentences in, her voice got this kind of musical thing. Did you know that was happening, Charlotte? Did you feel it?"

"Kinda."

"And the way she pretended to forget to say it was Jane Austen. She should get an Oscar. Did you notice the TV guy with the camera?"

Charlotte nodded.

"I'll bet you'll be on the news. We need to get home and look."

What had happened to James? All talky and fun again. The Return of the Alien Brother. Charlotte smiled to herself. Maybe all he needed was a punch in the nose.

When Charlotte saw herself on TV the only thing she could think of was that one piece of hair was sticking out over her left ear, like a little awning. She wanted to reach into the TV and cut it off. But it was also very interesting to see what she had missed and the camera had seen, like one of the school-board men laughing out loud.

"Hey! Was that O.O.?"

"Where?"

"Slipping out the door."

"Dang! Missed it."

"Look at Radger's face. Now that's scary."

It was. It flashed from surprised to pleased to furious.

"That was brilliant," said Dad. "I thought you were just planning to say what a good teacher O.O. was."

"And so poised," said Mom. "Wasn't she poised, Paul?"

It could actually have been a bit insulting, how surprised they were. But Charlotte didn't blame them. She was surprised, too. It was like the person on TV with the awning over her left ear was somebody else. Now that she was back to the original non-expando Charlotte though, all the attention was a little embarrassing.

At least it was all over. That was the thing about TV. It was there and then it was gone.

Wrong.

The first call was from Aunt Marlene. Then there were cousins and uncles and neighbors and Quakers and kids from school.

Then the local newspaper called with questions. How old was she? What grade was she in? Did she consider herself a typical thirteen-year-old? (What kind of a question was that?) Where did she get the idea? Charlotte found herself talking about Jerry Rubin and the Santa Claus outfit and then regretting it. Was she going to sound like a complete show-off?

Finally, had she really read *Pride and Prejudice*? That was the easy question. Yes, three times. What was the appeal of such an old-fashioned book? How was it relevant to the lives of today's teens?

"Jane Austen tells the truth."

All through the evening Charlotte kept checking her watch. If the Novaks drove straight up to Nelson and picked up Dawn and drove straight back …

No, they couldn't be home, not even with speeding.

She wanted Dawn to be home right now. She wanted her to never come home. She wanted to fire her as a friend. She wanted to patch it up, to get back to where they had been, to erase the fight. She wanted another fight except that this time she would be prepared and she'd win. She'd be really cool and precise and sarcastic. She'd make a proper fist with her voice. She'd say, "It's too bad you missed the school-board presentation. Do you recall that it was on Saturday? It went very well, as a matter of fact. But perhaps you had more pressing things to do."

She wanted … to stop talking to Dawn inside her head. She wanted to take a break from fame. She stumbled upstairs to bed with Puff winding around her every step.

Sixteen

How is Jane Austen relevant to the lives of today's teens?

Charlotte was home alone, dipping into *P&P.* She was looking for answers. Everyone else was at Meeting but she had slept in.

Dawn could be home by now. What if she phoned?

Charlotte thought about the newspaper interview. She should have told the reporter that Jane Austen understood about fights between friends.

Elizabeth and her best friend Charlotte (Charlotte!) didn't exactly have a fight, but after Charlotte got married things weren't quite the same, because she married a really pathetic guy. Elizabeth was always nice to her friend but things got tricky because they had such different ideas about marriage. Charlotte was pretty much one hundred percent ringy-dingy. Of course she had to be because of money. But when Elizabeth went to visit her it was just sad. It was maybe the saddest part of the book. But, because it was Jane Austen, it was also pretty funny.

Charlotte found the scene. Amazingly, the Jane Austen Charlotte seemed happy even though her husband was such a dork. She just liked having her own place. Elizabeth thought, *Her home and her housekeeping, her parish and her poultry, and all their dependent concerns, had not yet lost their charms.*

Poultry!

Charlotte checked the time again. Maybe Dawn would just turn up.

When Elizabeth tried to solve a problem she went into chess-player brain. If this, then that.

Maybe chess player was the way to go.

If Dawn came back all arrogant like Lydia then it would be impossible to be her friend. Wouldn't it?

If Dawn apologized for finking out of the school-board presentation then Charlotte could be just as generous as Elizabeth Bennet.

The ifs and thens started to circle in her brain.

If Tom Ed liked boys and Dawn liked him then ...

If you always thought you were one way and then you tried out being another way and discovered maybe you were a bit that way all along, was that fake or brave?

If you had a friend and she changed and you changed, too, but it made you not get along then were you maybe not really ever friends anyway?

The ring of the phone sent the questions scattering.

Dawn. Should she answer? Yes, no, yes, no, leap for the phone on the last ring.

It was somebody asking to speak to somebody called Lionel.

This was just ridiculous. She couldn't sort it out by thinking. She couldn't write a script with good lines for her because she had no idea what Dawn's lines would be. And she couldn't float along without it being sorted.

Dawn said, "Don't phone."

She didn't say, "Don't come over."

{I}

Charlotte stared up at Dawn's balcony on the fourth floor with its three perfectly placed pots of spring flowers.

What was she going to say? The only thing worse than ringing the intercom would be chickening out and going home. She pushed the button and said her name. There was a familiar blatting sound and the big glass door clicked open.

Somebody was moving furniture into the elevator.

Charlotte trudged up the four flights. Why was she here?

Dawn met her at their suite door. She called over her shoulder. "Charlotte's here. We're going to the locker."

On the stairs Dawn said only, "I'm grounded."

There wasn't much privacy in an apartment, but over the years Dawn and Charlotte had figured out places to go. Roof garden, laundry room, even the elevator. It was amazing how few people you saw in an apartment building, except at going-to-work and coming-home times.

One of the best places was the locker in the basement. It was secret and cozy. Mr. Novak had organized it like a little workshop, with tools and bottles of screws and stuff. Light slanted in from the hall through the slats and it had its own smell. Warm dust, cardboard, thrift store.

They sat on two boxes facing each other.

Dawn looked bad. She hadn't washed her hair and her pixie cut was greasy and clumpy.

"So. You probably told everyone, right?"

"What? No. Yesterday when some kids asked where you were I just said you were sick."

Yesterday. It was the perfect opening for Dawn to ask how the presentation had gone, the perfect opportunity for her to apologize.

But it was as if she was deaf.

"Oh. Okay. Thanks." The thanks came out all narrow and stiff.

Charlotte took a deep breath. The conversation was like a heavy boulder and it was obvious that she would have to push it up the hill.

"So. What happened up there?"

"What do you care? You just want to know about Tom, right?"

It was a punch to the stomach.

"No. I want to know what happened to you."

"Right. Sure. I know what this is all about. You think I don't know. You're like, oh, Dawn, she's not that smart. But I do know stuff. You had a thing for him yourself, didn't you? All that talking about books and listening to the Mothers of Invention. Faker. You wanted him for you."

Charlotte jumped off her box. Her feet were ahead of her brain.

"That's just *stupid*. You ..." She felt her throat squeezing and the words disappearing.

She tried to slam the door of the locker behind her but it had sticky hinges and barely closed. She kicked it into place and the walls of the lockers trembled.

Stamp, stamp, stamp, down the hall, stamp up the stairs and into the lobby. Hand on the front door and then ...

Dawn's a dope and she pushes you around too much.

No. Not this time. She wasn't going to give up. She wasn't going to wait for Dawn to get over it. She wasn't going to nice-nice her way back in.

Dawn was just leaving the locker. "Forget something?"

She kept moving down the hall toward Charlotte.

Charlotte flung her arm out. "Get back there. We're not finished."

Dawn stumbled back and blinked and the sneer on her face changed to something Charlotte couldn't quite read, but she turned and went back to the locker.

They both stayed standing, a fit as tight as an elevator.

"You wonder if I forgot something? Yeah! I did. I forgot to tell you about yesterday with the O.O. thing. Remember that? Remember how you were going to be the speaker? Remember how we had a plan? Did you think about that? But I guess you had other things on your mind. Like using *lines*. Here's what I don't get about that. Why would you take the advice of some mean flute player that you don't even like?"

Dawn opened her mouth to reply but Charlotte shook her head.

"No, you don't get to talk now. Tom *Ed*? Yes, I had a *thing* with him. It's called friends. We talked. It's what I used to have with you. Before you started to act like some stupid teenager. You know what? If you're quitting Unteen you could at least have warned me."

As it all spilled out, Charlotte felt her voice change. It was doing that thing from the O.O. presentation, getting bigger and deeper, filling every nook and cranny of the locker. She had absolutely no urge to throw up or cry.

"And, by the way, Dawn, if you want to tell a story to impress some *boy*, get your own. I was the one who wrote those essays on plywood, not you."

She pushed open the door. That was it. End of what she had to say.

End of Dawn as a friend, obviously.

"Plywood?"

The voice wasn't mad, just small and confused. Charlotte turned back to see Dawn sliding down the wall. She looked up and her eyes were big and round. Then they started to leak and her face melted. All the edges got blurry and trembly. Her cheeks were wet all over.

"Oh, Charlotte. It was awful. He was … he was embarrassed by me."

It was pretty much impossible to stay furious at a person whose face was melting, especially if you'd known that person nearly your whole life and even if she had been acting like a total jerk.

Charlotte took a deep breath and crouched down.

"So you did see him?"

"Yeah."

"How did you even find him? I thought you got, like, arrested as soon as you got off the bus."

"It was Annie."

Dawn gave a hiccuping gulp. She twisted around to reach the pocket of her sweatpants. She pulled out a ragged tissue and mopped her eyes.

"There was this woman named Annie. Youth worker. I went to her house for the night. Not jail. Anyway, she was really nice and she said that even though it wasn't procedure, as I had come all that way I should have a chance to see Tom."

"She knew him already?"

"No. But I remembered that name from the letter. Remember? Where you were supposed to send his check? V. Popoff. Annie knew them, Vern and Wendy. She said that most of the dodgers end up there to begin with. She had some stuff to drop off to Wendy so I could come along. We walked to this big old hippie-looking house and there he was right on the porch, playing a guitar. Did you even know he played the guitar?"

Charlotte shook her head.

"When I saw him something happened to my ears and all I could hear was the guitar. Like tunnel vision but for ears. I don't even know what happened to Annie. I got to the front gate, and then he saw me. Oh, Charlotte. He …"

Dawn's voice snipped off.

Charlotte rocked back and sat down on her bum. She let Dawn's report sink in.

Forget the formula. It was real. What Dawn felt for Tom Ed? It wasn't made up to show off. It was Juliet and Elizabeth and whatshername in *Love Story*.

Charlotte felt the whole story twisting into a new shape. How could Dawn feel like her best, oldest friend and a complete stranger all at the same time?

"He what?"

"I saw the whole thing go across his face. It was like, 'Oh, here's Dawn. What? What's Dawn doing here? Oh, no. Get me out of here.' And then back to yes ma'am polite and friendly. It was fast, fast, fast. I was a *problem*." Dawn's voice cracked.

"What happened then?"

"The happy hippies gave us lunch."

"What was Tom Ed like?"

"Friendly. Funny. Nice. Beautiful. Even though I saw what he thought about me it didn't change anything. I just wanted to be in the same room with him, breathing the same air. I know it's crazy but I feel exactly the same about him as before."

Dawn's voice rose toward a wail. "If only I was older. We did have something. I couldn't have made it all up. He *got* me. Maybe I wasn't smart enough. But I *was* smart with him. I liked me with him. No, it was me. I'm just wrong."

Dust motes moved through slats of light. Dawn abandoned the Kleenex and wiped her nose on the bottom of her shirt.

Charlotte made a decision.

"It isn't you."

"Huh?"

"I mean, it's you, but it isn't anything about being smart or right or old enough."

"What do you mean?"

"So Tuesday morning? I got up early. It was Puff …"

The story ended with the kiss.

Dawn blinked a few times and frowned, like somebody doing a hard math problem.

"Oh, they were probably just horsing around. Guys are always doing that, grabbing each other. Like on the football field or … Are you sure? "

"I'm sure. James talked to me about it. I think it might be why Tom Ed left in such a hurry."

Dawn still had her math face on. Math was an improvement over melting.

"So when I said he seemed like a person with a secret he might have thought I meant …"

"Yeah. Probably."

There was a long pause. Charlotte stared at the yellow-handled screwdrivers on the wall, big to little.

Dawn's voice was small. "I don't get it. He just doesn't seem … you know."

"Well, neither does James."

There was a sound from the main door to the locker area, a creak and a scrape.

"Shhhhh." They both had the same instinct, to hide as though they were doing something wrong. They froze and gave each other "yikes" looks.

The scrape came closer and then stopped at the locker right beside them. There was the clink of keys, more scraping accompanied by grunts and one inappropriate word. The shared wall shook as a box was slammed against it and then there were the sounds of retreat.

As the footsteps reached the main door there was a click, and all the lights went out.

There was a squeak from Dawn.

"Charlotte?"

"Yeah."

"I'm sorry about the presentation. I'm sorry I finked out on you."

In the light Charlotte would probably have tidied it all up and said something like, "Oh, that's okay," but in the pitch-dark it felt right to just say nothing.

"It would have been good."

"It *was* good."

"What? Who did it?"

"Me."

"No!"

"Yeah. I was on TV."

Darkness was also good for describing what it was like to be famous. Charlotte told the whole story in detail.

"Sounds like it worked. I bet O.O. will be back on Monday."

"Hope so. Bye-bye Blinker!"

"And … I've been thinking about the Unteen thing. Maybe next January when we have our birthdays we could decide to be quatorze instead of fourteen? You know, French and cool."

It was a peace offering. Dawn might have turned into a stranger in some ways but Charlotte could still read her. Was that what she wanted, though, to be cool in the way Dawn wanted to be cool? And next January was *months* away.

But a cupcake was a cupcake. Charlotte reached out with her voice into the darkness and accepted it.

"Maybe. Let's decide next year."

seventeen

O.O. was back in class on Monday morning with two more boxes of books to give away. She had been doing more weeding.

The term wound down with old books and new.

Larry moved on from pit bulls to the Hungarian Vizsla. Sylvia finished *The Lord of the Rings* but even 1008 pages didn't get her an A. Charlotte gave *P&P* a rest and brought in some of James's hand-me-down *Mad* magazines.

"Excellent introduction to the art of satire," said O.O.

At the end of the year there was a big retirement party for O.O. in the gym with teachers, parents, kids and former students, including James. O.O. gave a funny speech in which she revealed that she was planning to write a book. She was secretive about the subject, just the way a former spy would be.

Nothing more was heard from Bernice Radger or Dorcas.

The year rolled to a close. There was elementary school "graduation." Charlotte thought it was dumb and fake. Dawn said she did, too, but she still got her hair done at a hairdresser.

As summer began, Charlotte got lots of babysitting work with the Seeleys, including going away with them to their swanky summer cabin.

"Why do they need a babysitter when they're both there?" asked Dad.

Mom rolled her eyes. "Because with small children you're never really there even when you're there. Your mouth is saying things about, say, Leonard Bernstein but your mind is actually taken up with questions such as what did the baby just put in her nose."

"Leonard Bernstein?" said Dad. "Who's talking about Leonard Bernstein?"

"I imagine the Seeleys discuss serious music. You know, with their high-falutin' friends."

Charlotte smiled. The Seeleys and their friends were actually quite low-falutin'. They talked about shopping.

It was a great job. Charlotte mastered a couple of valuable life skills such as water-skiing and how to make martinis. She got a tan and she earned a bucket of lovely money.

Nevertheless, by the time three weeks were over she had had it with small children, even adorable ones.

Dawn went back to the old country with her parents to visit her grandparents and what sounded like dozens of cousins who all seemed to be called Luka or Mia. She sent jokey postcards signed Ringo Starr or Chairman Mao.

James decided to switch from Commerce to Computer Science. He was still trying to convince the family that money made the world go round rather than love, peace, understanding and houseplants, but he changed his tune to include money *and* computers. Charlotte paid close attention to his reports of his social life but as far as she could tell his friends were friends and not boyfriends.

Uncle Claude and Gloria took the Fun Bus to Reno.

Summer, which began slow, speeded up as always and then, boom, it was September and high school. There were lockers and timetables, a science lab, halls that thundered between classes and a choice of electives. There were clubs. Dawn joined junior string orchestra and Charlotte decided to give drama a try.

The drama club kids were all new to Charlotte, from other schools and in all different grades. They were friendly in an easy way and even hung out together at lunch sometimes. The older ones, who had been in productions before, could have whole conversations using lines from the plays. One would say, "Everybody's got an ism these days," and that would start them all off and then everyone would crack up. There was a lot of talk about cast parties.

At first Charlotte thought she would just learn about lighting or help with props or costumes but around the end of September they picked a play to work on and it happened to have a kid character, eleven years old. Charlotte was the only grade eight girl in the drama club and the smallest. They all said she should try out. Officially she said she was still thinking about it, but secretly she had already learned all the lines and acted out the whole thing for Puff.

There was no news of Tom Ed and it started to seem like he had been a play all on his own, with its own dialogue and props and blocking and a final curtain. But then one evening Uncle Claude made a dessert called sticky toffee pudding (very popular with lumberjacks) and the sticky toffee pulled out one of Charlotte's fillings. The dental appointment had to be the next morning early and by the time Charlotte got home with a frozen mouth she decided not to go back to school.

She was alone in the house, lying on the chesterfield exploring her new filling with her tongue when the mail thunked through the door.

At first she didn't recognize the messy handwriting on the envelope. *Miss Charlotte Quintan.* Bad handwriting, but formal.

Then she remembered where she had seen it before.

Dear Charlotte,

Remember when we talked about courage? And I told you how JJ said courage doesn't have anything to do with throwing yourself into battle, but that real courage is just standing in place, holding the space for the next person?

I didn't do that. I didn't stay in place. I should have tried to sort it out with James. But I was a chicken. I panicked and deserted.

I wrote to James to try to make that right.

But I'm writing to you too just to say I miss you. Lots has happened to me since last spring. For the first while I lived in a tent and got a job tree planting. Then I moved into a commune. That's like a family of people that you're not related to. We built a footbridge across a river. We got a grant for that work and the money will go toward getting our own school one day.

The folks in the commune want to change the world, get rid of private ownership and war. There are some babies and little kids (on squares one and two!) and we're going to make a good world for them. Because of Canada, I have the chance to live the rest of my life and not end up dead in some jungle so I'm determined to make it a good one, to do the right thing.

We have kind neighbors. There's these people called Douk-hobors. They are pacifists, like Quakers, and they bring us bread and vegetables and teach us about growing food and canning and such. They also believe in dramatic protest. One of their protest things from a few years ago was walking around naked! Wonder what Mrs. Radger would have thought of that!

The people in our commune are also about telling people when you love them. So here goes.

Charlotte Quintan, I love you. I love how smart you are and how thoughtful. I love how you jump right into a joke, doing a cannonball. I love how you go loop-di-loop with an idea. I love it that there are some games you don't play. And some you do. I love how you did that thing at the school board. I saw your picture in the paper. ~~If I had a kid sister.~~ No, that's not the whole of it. If I ever meet a boy who's just like you, or like you're going to be when you grow up into

177

an astonishing adult I'm going to wrestle him to the ground
and hog–tie him so he can't get away ever.
Love to you, Charlotte Q.,
Tom Ed.

Charlotte leaned against the wall and slid down until she was sitting on the floor. She read the letter again. A third time and his voice came into the room, his slow drawly way of speaking that turned words into elastic bands.

"Wrastle im to the ground uhn hog-tah im."

He had remembered so much. Hopscotch and Mrs. Radger and everything.

And so. Did this count as a love letter? Did she feel crushy? There *was* a kind of happy-sad thing going on that felt new.

Mostly, though, the letter made her feel like fresh air was blowing through her brain. It was all even more complicated than Juliet and Elizabeth would lead you to expect.

Tom Ed did not write that letter to a kid. He even crossed out "kid sister." And he wouldn't have sent it to an adult because that would lead to all kinds of misunderstandings.

So maybe there was something to be said for being a square five teenager after all. Maybe the answer was to create a version of square five all your own — square 5A or square cinq or $\sqrt{5}$.

Charlotte stretched out her legs and read the letter one more time. Loop-di-loop with an idea.

Hmmm. Do-it-yourself square five.

Maybe she had already started.

Who Were the Draft Dodgers?

The draft is a system in which citizens are obliged to serve in the military. Not many countries have a draft now but in the 1960s and 70s the United States drafted young men, aged eighteen to twenty-five, to fight a war in the Southeast Asian country of Vietnam.

On one side of the Vietnam War was Communist North Vietnam, supported by Communist nations such as China and the Soviet Union. On the other side was South Vietnam, supported by the anti-Communist United States. The leader of North Vietnam wanted a united, independent country. The United States wanted to prevent the spread of Communism in Asia.

Over the course of twenty years the United States spent about $168 billion on the war. By the time it was over, 50,000 Americans and millions of Vietnamese had been killed. In the end, the U.S. pulled out, and North and South Vietnam united.

Many young Americans were against the war. They thought it was foolish, unnecessary and immoral.

For some young men the only way to avoid military service was to run away to another country. Canada was the obvious choice. Nobody is sure how many draft dodgers came to Canada, but it was probably about 30,000. The war ended in 1975, and in 1977 the draft dodgers were pardoned, meaning they could go home again. But by then, many had put down roots and considered Canada home.

With thanks to Bill Bargeman, Eric Harms and Tom Sandborn, dodger boys who shared their stories with me.

With thanks to the Canada Council for the Arts.

SARAH ELLIS is a celebrated author, teacher and children's literature expert. She has written more than twenty books across the genres, and her books have been translated into French, Spanish, Danish, Chinese and Japanese. She has won the Governor General's Literary Award (*Pick-Up Sticks*), the TD Canadian Children's Literature Award (*Odd Man Out*) and the Sheila A. Egoff Children's Literature Prize. Her first novel, *The Baby Project*, remains a children's classic, still in print more than thirty years after publication.

Sarah is a masthead reviewer for the *Horn Book Magazine*, and she is a former faculty member at Vermont College of Fine Arts. She lives in Vancouver.